W9-AUI-985

Truth and Kisses

December 31, 5:45 p.m.

I can't decide if the year is ending horribly or if what just occurred an omen of the next one beginning like crap. It's probably both.

My problems started last week when Mom showed May, June, and m the dresses she'd made for us to wear to Gaga's wedding, which is tonight. "Gaga chose the color," said Mom. "Eggplant is a lovely shade of purple," she added, like it was a little-known fact that might convince me the dress isn't hideous.

"I think it looks like something you'd find in a bin at the farmer's market," I said.

But Mom kept talking like it was a done deal. "You girls will look so pretty at the wedding." Apparently, picturing us in our veggie-inspired getups was enough to make her happy.

I didn't want to be the one to burst her happy bubble, but I didn't have a choice. It's bad enough that I have to go to my eighty-year-old grandmother's wedding on New Year's Eve, but it's completely unacceptable that Mom thought I'd show up wearing the same thing as my seven- and ten-year-old sisters. Two words: Ain't Happenin

I looked at the pile of shiny fabric like it was a dead cockroach. "I'm not wearing matching dresses."

Mom eyeballed me in her don't-be-ridiculous way. "I thought you'd sa something like that. Look, they're different styles. I just made them the same material so they coordinate."

Seriously? Did Mom really think coordinating eggplant dresses are better than matching ones? Whatever. That was a week ago, and right now I'd give anything to be wearing the dress she made.

Truth and Kisses

LAURIE FRIEDMAN

Darby Creek
A division of Lerner Publishing Group, Inc.
241 First Avenue North
Minneapolis, MN 55401 USA

For reading levels and more information, look up this title at www.lernerbooks.com.

Main body text set in Janson Text LT Std 12/17.
Typeface provided by Linotype AG.

Library of Congress Cataloging-in-Publication Data

Friedman, Laurie B., 1964–
Truth and kisses / by Laurie Friedman.
pages cm. — (The mostly miserable life of April Sinclair ; #3)
Summary: Diary entries reveal thirteen-year-old April Sinclair's complicated best-friend/love triangle, her new friendship, a busy dance team schedule, and a closer relationship with Matt Parker that surprises her and everyone else.
ISBN 978-1-4677-0927-9 (trade hard cover ; alk. paper)
ISBN 978-1-4677-4648-9 (eBook)
[1. Friendship—Fiction. 2. Dating (Social customs)—Fiction. 3. Interpersonal relations—Fiction. 4. Dance teams—Fiction. 5. Diaries—Fiction.] I. Title.
PZ7.F89773Tru 2014
[Fic]—dc23 2013045913

Manufactured in the United States of America
1 – BP – 7/15/14

For Anna Cavallo, editor extraordinaire!
With all my thanks,
L.B.F.

And special thanks to Alondra, Carmen, Natalia, Grace Lily, and Isabella at Nativity School in Hollywood and Mia, Calypso, Gabrielle, Luna, Karina, Katerina, and Wendi at Miami Country Day.

We don't know where it will lead.
We just know there's something much
bigger than any of us here.

—*Steve Jobs*

December 31, 5:45 p.m.

I can't decide if the year is ending horribly or if what just occurred is an omen of the next one beginning like crap. It's probably both.

My problems started last week when Mom showed May, June, and me the dresses she'd made for us to wear to Gaga's wedding, which is tonight. "Gaga chose the color," said Mom. "Eggplant is a lovely shade of purple," she added, like it was a little-known fact that might convince me the dress isn't hideous.

"I think it looks like something you'd find

in a bin at the farmer's market," I said.

But Mom kept talking like it was a done deal. "You girls will look so pretty at the wedding." Apparently, picturing us in our veggie-inspired getups was enough to make her happy.

I didn't want to be the one to burst her happy bubble, but I didn't have a choice. It's bad enough that I have to go to my eighty-year-old grandmother's wedding on New Year's Eve, but it's completely unacceptable that Mom thought I'd show up wearing the same thing as my seven- and ten-year-old sisters. Two words: *Ain't. Happenin'*.

I looked at the blur of shiny fabric like it was a dead cockroach. "I'm not wearing matching dresses."

Mom eyed me in her don't-be-ridiculous way. "I thought you'd say something like that. Look, they're different styles—just made from the same material so they coordinate."

Seriously? Did Mom really think coordinating eggplant dresses are better than matching ones? Whatever. That was a week ago, and right now I'd give anything to be wearing the dress she made, because what I'm currently wearing is so much worse. Thanks to May, a "last-minute wardrobe change" (Brynn's phrase) was required.

Brynn made it sound glamorous, like something that might happen on a Hollywood movie set, but it wasn't like that. When Brynn came over this afternoon to help me with my hair and makeup (which I was happy about because she's awesome with both), I asked May to get the curling iron out of her room and plug it in.

Brynn and I went in the bathroom, and she got out some of the makeup she'd brought over to get started on my face. "I think we should go for smoky eyes and sun-kissed skin." She applied bronzer to my cheeks. "It'll look good with your dress," she said.

"Nothing will look good with my dress," I said.

Brynn made a *hmmm* sound. "We'll make your hair and makeup look so good, no one will even notice the dress." She smiled at me in the mirror, and I smiled back. Even though she was being her brutally honest self and had just acknowledged that the dress was actually as bad as I thought it was, she was sweet to help me. I knew she was doing her best to be a good friend.

I closed my eyes, and Brynn had just started putting shadow on my lids when we first smelled it. "Is something burning?" she asked.

I inhaled. "Mom must be cooking." In my family, Dad is the cook.

Brynn continued with mascara. Then she stopped. I opened my eyes and saw her fanning the air in front of her nose. "It smells like it's coming from your room."

Right when she said that, we heard a blood-curdling screech. And then another.

"APRIL'S ROOM IS ON FIRE!" yelled May.

"APRIL'S ROOM IS ON FIRE!" repeated June, who, I have to admit, for the first time in her life, had finally found something worth repeating.

Brynn dropped the mascara wand, and we ran into my room.

After that, everything spun together. Flames were shooting up from the top of my dresser.

Mom ran into my room. Dad wasn't far behind with the fire extinguisher. The next thing I knew, my dresser was covered with charred shreds of eggplant-colored satin, a smoking curling iron, and extinguisher foam. Dad was beside himself. Mom wasn't exactly happy either. "April, how could you leave a curling iron plugged in on top of your dress? You know it's synthetic!" she scolded.

I shot a look at my mom. Who clothes their daughters in material that's a fire hazard? Then I turned to the real culprit. "Why are you yelling at me? May was the one who put the curling iron there." My parents' eyes fixed on her.

May pointed at me. "April told me to do it."

My parents looked at June, like they actually expected a seven-year-old to act as referee in this situation. Which she did. "Yeah," said June. "I heard April tell her to do it."

Dad slumped down on my bed and clutched his chest like he was having a heart attack. Then the questions started flying. *April, why didn't you check to be sure the curling iron was plugged in safely? April, do you have any idea what could have happened? April, how could you be so irresponsible?* He asked all kinds of questions except the most important one.

"WHAT AM I GOING TO WEAR TONIGHT?" I moaned.

Dad blinked like that was the last thing on his mind.

Mom, to her credit, actually sprang into action. But unfortunately, the answer to my question is a disastrous mix of color-correct items including purple tights, a purple stretchy miniskirt from sixth grade that I have pulled down as low as possible so my butt doesn't hang out the back, a purple cardigan of May's with a Nick Jr. logo on it that Mom covered up with a fake purple flower pin she made, and some purple felt and curtain rope that she twisted together and wrapped around my waist like a belt. I look like a craft project that just walked out of Michael's. I didn't even have to ask Brynn what she thought. The look on her face said it all.

God help me tonight—since no amount of makeup will.

1:08 a.m.

Back from Gaga's wedding.

Tonight was more like a *Saturday Night Live* skit than a wedding.

Every single female in my extended family was wearing eggplant. My mom and her sisters all had on the same long, flowy dresses. They looked like bridesmaids gone terribly wrong. My cousins Amanda, Charlotte, and Izzy were dressed in eggplant skirts and sweater sets.

When Amanda saw me, she frowned.

"What's your problem?" I asked. But I didn't hang around for an explanation. The answer was obvious.

As I looked around the room, I couldn't believe what I was seeing. The ladies weren't the only ones sporting the color theme. The men had on purple ties that Gaga and her groom, Willy Sherman, had bought online. They were more electric purple than eggplant, and Gaga was upset they didn't match the color swatch she'd gotten, but Willy assured her that they looked like something the British monarchy would wear. I don't know which gossip mags he reads, but I'd never seen Wills or Harry or any other royal wearing anything like that. Gaga and Willy were also in eggplant, from head to toe—for better or worse (wedding humor). The rest of the room was purple too. Flowers. Candles. Tablecloths. You name it. It looked like someone had projectile vomited grape juice all over the place.

Our family wasn't the only group there to witness my fashion humiliation. All of Gaga's lady friends from the Happiness Movement were there, in eggplant, and so was Willy's family. He actually doesn't have much family—just one daughter, who's married and lives in New York City and was there with her husband and their daughter, Sophie.

When Sophie walked in, Amanda came over to me and whispered, "She looks like a supermodel." Amanda's only in sixth grade, but it was an accurate observation. Somehow Sophie actually rocked the eggplant look, if that's possible. "She's probably totally not normal," added Amanda, whose latest thing is trying to psychoanalyze people.

I shook my head. "You can't tell by looking at someone," I said. But the truth was, I'd never seen anyone who looked like Sophie. She had pale skin, long black hair, and violet eyes.

"Do you think her mother let her buy colored contacts for the wedding?" Amanda asked.

From the looks of her mom, it seemed possible. She was even more chic than her daughter. She had on a long eggplant skirt, a sheer black top, ropes of black beads around her neck, and high-heeled boots. Sophie was wearing a short-skirt version of her mother's outfit. Both of them had their eyelids done in dark, smoky eye shadow. As good as Brynn is at makeup, what she did to me couldn't compare to how good their makeup looked. They must have had it professionally done.

When Willy introduced Sophie to us, I just stood there like an idiot, staring at her. Even though he said Sophie and I are the same age, I had no clue what to say to her.

The good news is that I didn't stand there for too long looking mute, because Gaga announced it was time to start the ceremony, which fortunately was quick. When the justice of the peace asked Gaga and Willy if they vowed to love each other for as long as they both shall live, Gaga said, "It won't be all that long because we're so damn old." Then she said she didn't want to waste another minute, grabbed Willy, and kissed him long and hard on the lips, and the justice of the peace pronounced them husband and wife.

"That's repulsive," muttered my cousin Harry.

"I'm scarred for life," said Amanda.

I didn't respond. What more was there to say? Everything about watching my eighty-year-old grandmother make out with her new husband was just so wrong. After the ceremony, there was a reception, and everyone made toasts to Gaga and Willy. Most of them were pretty forgettable. I guess there aren't that many ways to congratulate octogenarians who hook up. Willy's toast to Gaga was memorable, though. He told her how much he loves her, and then he said all her grandkids could call him Grandpa Willy.

"Sounds like a perv," whispered Harry.

It's a definite possibility.

When Willy was done, Gaga made a toast to him. She tapped her spoon against her champagne glass until the room was quiet. "I wanted to get married on New Year's Eve so I could start the year off right." Gaga raised her glass and gazed lovingly (two words I've never used in conjunction with each other and never thought I would, especially in a case like this) at Willy. "Today is the first day of the rest of our lives." They clinked glasses and kissed again.

"Yuck," said Harry.

Then Gaga launched into a long speech about the importance of making a New Year's resolution and sticking to it. "My resolution is to live every day like it matters," she announced, slowly and loudly, enunciating each word, like we all might be deaf and she wanted to be sure we got how she plans to spend her time.

I thought the reception should have been winding down at that point, but Gaga said it was time to dance. There was a band (if you want to call it that). But there wasn't anyone to dance with, unless my dad or Harry counted (which they don't). So I was left standing there, trying to look like I was enjoying myself, until the clock struck midnight, when Gaga said we would throw confetti while she and Willy made their departure. Luckily, Sophie came over and started talking to me. "So this is what weddings are like in Faraway?" she asked.

"It's the first wedding I've ever been to." I wondered if it sounded babyish to admit that, but Sophie was nodding her head.

"This is my first wedding too." She paused like she was trying to decide if it was a good or bad idea to say what she was about to. "How weird is it that your grandmother and my grandfather just got married?"

I stood there with my mouth open. She had taken the words right out of it. "So weird!"

Sophie twirled a strand of beads around her finger. "So what does that make us, like, step-grand cousins?"

I wasn't actually sure. "Something like that."

Sophie grinned.

I was trying to figure out what to say next.

What I really felt like doing was explaining why I was wearing such a ridiculous outfit. I didn't want Sophie to think I always dressed like this, but before I could say a word she launched into her personal history. Born in France. Dad from Paris. Lived there until a few months ago, when she moved to New York City. I wanted to find out more, but Gaga broke up the party and made us dance. When the clock struck twelve, we all screamed "*Happy New Year!*" and threw confetti as Gaga and Willy left to start the rest of their lives together.

The whole night was surreal. I never expected to start the year off at my eighty-year-old grandmother's wedding or that I'd have a new supermodel-slash-step-grand cousin.

It makes a girl wonder: What does the rest of the year have in store?

Much unhappiness has come into the world because of bewilderment and things left unsaid.

—Dostoyevsky

New Year's Day
Off to a bad start

The first word I should be writing today is *happy*, as in "Happy New Year!" But the year's not starting off so happy. Brynn just called and was like, "Get over here ASAP! My mom said I could have a New Year's getty at my house. It's going to be so much fun. I'm calling Billy when we hang up, and then I'm calling a bunch of other people. I'm super excited!"

I was super excited too, but when I went into the kitchen and asked Mom if I could go to

Brynn's getty, here's what happened:

> Mom: "Getty" isn't a word.
>
> Me (Patiently): Get-together. May I please go to Brynn's today for a get-together?
>
> Mom: We're going to be spending the day with family.
>
> Me (Not as patiently): We spent last night with family.
>
> Mom (Looking confused): Your point is?
>
> Me (No longer patient): I was with my family last night, which happened to be New Year's Eve. Is it so hard to understand that I want to spend New Year's Day with my friends?

Apparently it was, for Mom, because she went on a long rant about how I shouldn't start the year off with such a fresh mouth and that Gaga only gets married once.

I corrected Mom. "This makes twice."

Mom said that wasn't the point. "April, your family is spending the day together at Gaga's house, eating brunch and watching football.

Since you're part of the family, that's what you'll be doing too."

I often wonder if I was one of those sad cases of babies who are switched at birth and end up with the wrong family. Today I'm almost sure of it.

6:42 p.m.

I can't decide if today was more good or bad. It was definitely some of both. The good part was that Sophie was at Gaga's, and I hung out with her all day. She's really cool. When I got there, Sophie was nowhere in sight. I thought it was going to be just another long day at Gaga's listening to Harry complaining and Amanda trying to analyze people. Gaga had a huge buffet laid out. I loaded my plate with eggs, bacon, biscuits, and what Dad calls his "world famous" cinnamon rolls from the Love Doctor Diner. I was on my way to sit in the den with my cousins when Sophie materialized. (That sounds unnecessarily *Twilight*-ish, but it was kind of like that.)

"We should eat outside," she said. I glanced at her plate. It was piled high with eggs and cinnamon rolls too. She didn't look like the kind of girl who would eat that stuff, but I was glad to see she was.

"It's pretty cold out there." I pretend-shivered.

Sophie laughed. "I'm from New York. This isn't cold." She started walking toward the patio like there was nothing about an Alabama winter day that scared her. I followed and sat down beside her. "So what's it like to live in this little town?" she asked.

Even though I'd be the first to admit it has never been my dream to live in Faraway, Alabama, part of me didn't want to make it seem so bad. "It's small," I told Sophie. "But there are some cool things about it."

Sophie raised a brow like she wanted me to elaborate.

"There are beaches nearby." I had to think while I talked. "You can walk just about anywhere, and there's an awesome ice cream place in the middle of town called The Cold Shack that Brynn and I always go to."

I waited for Sophie to say something like, *"That's the best you got?"*

"Who's Brynn?" she asked.

"My best friend since kindergarten." It was kind of hard to decide what else I wanted to tell Sophie about Brynn, but she kept munching on her cinnamon roll and not saying anything, so I kept going. "She's an only child, so in a way, we're more like sisters than friends."

"But you have sisters." Sophie had met May and June last night, and May had tried to pick her up, which is what she does when she meets people, and June stood there laughing like a crazy person while she did it. So I was pretty sure Sophie would understand how I felt about them.

"OK, Brynn is more like a sister I like."

Sophie laughed. "Your sisters are cute." I smiled. I'm not sure she meant it, but it was nice of her to say it. "So, are you and Brynn, like, the tell-each-other-everything kind of friends?"

I took a deep breath. I'd just met Sophie and I didn't want to tell her what Brynn and I have been through, especially over the past year. But Sophie just sat there, patiently eating forkful after forkful of scrambled eggs, and the story somehow spilled out. All of it.

I told her about Billy kissing me last spring, and then Matt, my hot new neighbor, kissing me, and how Brynn got mad when she heard about Matt and said some stuff that made me wonder if maybe she liked Billy. And how that was just before they went to camp together, without me.

Sophie raised a brow. "Wow," she said.

I nodded. "There's more. Billy and I got together when he came home from camp, and things were great, but then I made the high school dance team and Brynn . . . kind of . . . had a hard time with that." I paused. I wasn't quite sure what I wanted to say next.

Sophie smiled like she had ESP or somehow understood that things might have gotten complicated without me having to say it. She sat without saying a word until I started again.

I told her about Matt kissing me again and how it changed everything because it was so intense, and how I felt horrible about what I'd done to Billy, but I couldn't stop thinking about Matt.

"Juicy!" Sophie said, and laughed.

I smiled. I felt a little weird telling Sophie what happened, but she wasn't making any faces like she was judging me. "I knew I couldn't tell Brynn about Matt. Things had been weird between us because of dance, plus there were still signs that made me think she liked Billy. So I told this girl Emily, on the dance team, instead, but then she told everyone, and before I knew it, my life fell apart."

I confided in Sophie about Billy breaking up with me, and how Brynn said she couldn't trust me anymore and that for a long time, the girls on the dance team weren't talking to me. I exhaled when I finished. It had been so horrible when it happened, but it felt oddly easy to tell Sophie about it.

"So who do you like? Billy or Matt?" she asked when I was done.

I hadn't thought about it like that. "I'm not sure," I said honestly.

Sophie laughed. "TBD," she said.

It was time to change the subject. "So what about you? Living in Paris must have been cool."

Sophie flashed a huge grin when I said that.

"Paris is great. I didn't want to move, but my dad got this big job." She paused. "I hated leaving all my friends behind in Paris, but I like New York. I go to an art school, which is pretty cool. I want to be a painter."

It definitely sounded cool. "They don't even have schools like that in Faraway."

Sophie nodded. "When I turn eighteen, I'm going to get a tiny butterfly tattoo right above my ankle bone." She lifted the leg of her jeans and showed me where it would go. "I love butterflies," said Sophie. "They represent lightness, beauty, and freedom."

I was overwhelmed just listening to her. I've never thought about what things like butterflies represent, and I certainly haven't done any planning for what I'm going to do when I turn eighteen. I think Sophie mistook my silence as judgment, because she kind of shrugged and changed her tone and said, "I just think butterflies are very Zen, and I like that idea. Know what I mean?"

I nodded like I got it, even though I wasn't sure I did.

When we finished eating, Sophie's parents said they had to leave. "We're flying back to New York tomorrow, but we should keep in touch," she said.

"I'd love that," I told her as we put each other's numbers into our phones. It was cool that she wanted to be friends. I was in a good mood the rest of the day at Gaga's, and I was still happy as we were driving home. I even laughed when May and June, prompted by the reminder Gaga had given as we left her house, made their New Year's resolutions.

"My New Year's resolution is to eat chocolate every day," said May.

"My New Year's resolution is to eat chocolate every day too," said June.

I tickled her ribs and called her by her nickname, which came from one of her favorite books when she was little. "Silly Sally, you have to make your own resolution."

June thought for a minute. "My New Year's resolution is to eat vanilla every day."

Everyone laughed, even June, who didn't really get why we were laughing. Dad looked in the rearview mirror in my direction. "April, what's your resolution?"

I shook my head. "TBD," I told Dad.

I was still on a high when I got home, but that ended when I went to my room and called Brynn. "How was the getty?" I asked.

Brynn paused for a beat too long before she answered. "It didn't really work out."

"That's too bad." I actually did feel bad for her since she'd been so excited about having people over when she called me earlier that morning.

"No big deal," said Brynn. Then she made this weird sigh, like she was trying to decide exactly how to put what she said next. "It was hard to get people to come over at the last minute, so it was just Billy and me."

I didn't respond. Brynn continued. "He's still here, and we're hanging out on my bed watching the end of a movie." I heard laughter. "Can I call you when he leaves?"

"Sure," I said like it was no big deal.

But it was.

7:22 p.m.

Should I be annoyed that Billy and Brynn spent the day together, alone?

Well . . . I am. I'm going to take a bath and try to get un-annoyed. It seems like a Zen way to handle things.

8:49 p.m.

Least Zen bath ever

I must be the only teen in America who has ever gotten in trouble while taking a bath.

I was in the tub trying to relax, but I couldn't stop thinking about Brynn and Billy. I think Brynn actually planned to spend the day alone with him. Maybe it wasn't her initial plan, but when she called me and I said I couldn't come over, she probably decided that instead of having other people over, she'd just invite Billy so they could spend the day together. Usually it wouldn't bother me so much, but it does after what also happened the other day when Brynn got back from her ski trip. She had Billy and me over, and it was totally weird.

When I got to Brynn's house that day, Billy

was there too. She had brought back presents for both of us, but I think she only brought back something for me so she'd have an excuse to give him something.

"April, I'm so happy to see you!" Brynn said. Her voice was overly sweet, like cotton candy or Skittles. Then she put one arm around me and another one around Billy. "I could hardly wait for you guys to get here. I brought back amazing stuff."

Even though we've all been friends for so long, it was strangely uncomfortable sitting there with Brynn in the middle and her arms around both of us, waiting to be given our gifts.

"You first," Brynn said pointing to me. She handed me a wrapped box. "You're. Going. To. Love. It!" She enunciated each word like there was something really special in the box. But when I opened it, the only thing inside was a T-shirt that said *I skied Aspen Mountain.* It was nice that Brynn brought me back a T-shirt, but since I hadn't skied Aspen Mountain, it would look kind of stupid if I wore it and someone asked me about it.

"Thanks!" I tried to pretend that I liked the shirt, but Brynn wasn't paying attention to me anymore.

She was already focused on Billy. "I hope you like what I brought you." She smiled as she handed him a different box, and she leaned in toward him while he opened it. When he pulled the lid off, I thought I was seeing things. "It's hand knit," Brynn said as Billy pulled out a beautiful sweater. She took it from him and held it up against him. "I picked this shade of blue because it matches your eyes." She steered Billy over to the mirror so he could see what she was talking about.

"Thanks," Billy said stiffly. What he didn't say was that it's weird she brought him back a fancy sweater or that it looks like something his mother would have bought for him. I could tell he wasn't sure what to do.

"Try it on," said Brynn.

Billy pulled his sweater on over his head. "It's great," he told Brynn.

She smiled at him and opened a drawer in her dresser and pulled out a similar sweater in pale pink. "I got one too."

Then, Brynn took off the sweatshirt she was wearing. All she had on was a white tank top and a bra and you could see her cleavage popping out of her tank top. She looked at Billy like she was curious if he noticed her like that. Honestly, it would have been hard not to. I'm sure Billy was thinking what I was thinking, which was that Brynn's boobs have gotten huge.

I looked away quickly. It would seem weird if she thought I was looking at her, but it was like she'd forgotten I was in the room. She pulled her sweater on. "Do you like the way this looks on me?" she tilted her head to the side while she waited for Billy's response.

He did this weird half-shrug. "It's nice," he said.

Brynn beamed, then she turned her attention back to me. "I would have gotten one for you too, but I thought you would say it was itchy."

She said it like that explained why she brought Billy back a hand-knit sweater and me a T-shirt. But that made no sense because in the history of my friendship with Brynn, I've never once complained about a sweater being itchy.

Tonight in the bathtub, I was thinking about why in the world a girl would give a guy, even a best-friend guy, a sweater when May and June started banging on the bathroom door.

"April, time's up!" yelled May.

"Yeah, it's our turn!" screamed June. They kept banging and yelling and the lock was moving like they were trying to stick something in it so they could get the door open.

"GO AWAY!" I yelled at the top of my lungs.

Then I suppose I did yell some other stuff about them being the most annoying little sisters on the planet, and the next thing I knew, Mom knocked on the door and said, "April, I don't like what you're saying or the tone you're saying it in. This is NOT a good way to start the new year!"

Well, that's one thing we can agree on. I don't think the year has started off so well either. I talked to Brynn over an hour ago, and she still hasn't called me back. I don't know if it's because Billy is still there and she can't or if it's because he's gone and she doesn't want to. Maybe she and Billy are like Gaga and Willy—today is the first day of the rest of their lives. I know that sounds overly dramatic, but my brain is picturing them laughing and talking and lying on her bed watching movies. I keep thinking about what Brynn's boobs looked like in that tank top. I hope Billy hasn't been thinking about the same thing.

Dear God, please don't let Billy have spent New Year's Day thinking about Brynn's boobs.

9:58 p.m.
Still upset

I know if I asked Brynn why she only had Billy over today, she'd say they've been friends forever so of course she wanted to spend New Year's Day with him, and that she invited other people (including me) but no one else could come. But it's so obvious how she really feels. They bonded over what Brynn called my "betrayal" when I kissed Matt, and she's happy about that. She brought him back a hand-knit sweater from her trip. And today, instead of having the getty that she was "super excited" about, she invited him over and they hung out on her bed watching movies.

She won't admit to me that she likes Billy,

but I know she does and that she wants to get together with him. I have no idea if he feels the same way. But I know this: I don't want Brynn to be with Billy. I want to be the one with him.

At the wedding, Gaga said it's important to make a resolution to start the year off right. She made a resolution to live each day like it matters. I don't usually agree with Gaga, but maybe that's what I need to do too—make a resolution, something that really matters to me, not something small like eating chocolate. The more I think about it, the more I know that's exactly what I need to do.

So here goes. I resolve to get Billy back.

How can you do push-ups when your nose gets in the way?

—Snoopy

Monday, January 6, 1:45 p.m.
Study Hall

I'm up to 434 quotes in my collection. I've always liked this one because it just seems so obvious. How can you be expected to do a push-up with a big, fat honker in the middle of your face? It's kind of like: How can you be expected to work right when you come back from winter break? Don't teachers get that your mind is still in hibernation mode?

Apparently not. This morning in science, Mrs. Thompson asked us if we'd had a nice break, and before anyone could even answer, she put up a chart about rain and frogs and started asking questions about the relationship between the amount of spring rainfall recorded over a five-year period and the number of frogs in the pond. Seriously? Who cares about rain or frogs or ponds?

Or the school newspaper?

Today at lunch, I was sitting with Billy and Brynn, and Brynn was talking to Billy about the paper like I wasn't even there. "As editor, I get to pick one student who makes a difference at school and do a feature story on that student."

"Interesting," said Billy.

I didn't think it was so interesting. I took a bite of my tuna wrap. Brynn smiled like she was glad Billy liked the idea. "Since you're president of the student body, I want to do the story on you." Whole-wheat tortilla stuck in my throat. I tried to swallow while I waited for Billy's response, which I thought was going to be something like *"Cool! I'd love for you to do that."*

But he surprised me. "I'm not sure the student body would be interested in me just because

I'm president." I looked at Brynn. Her face fell. I breathed a sigh of victory relief. But Billy wasn't done. "You'd have to find an angle that would be interesting to everyone," he said.

Brynn perked up and smiled again. "I'll think on it," she said. I got up and dumped the rest of my wrap in the trash. All I can say is, I hope Brynn finds other things to "think on."

6:08 p.m.
In the kitchen

I just got home from dance practice, which started up again tonight, and it was great. It was really fun to see all the girls on the team. Even Emily. After what happened last semester, I didn't think we'd ever be friends. We're really not, but we're not enemies either. It's like we declared a truce and we're more like fake friends, which is fine. After school ended today, Emily, Kate, Vanessa, and I all walked to the high school together, just like in the fall. When we got there, everyone was hugging and in a good mood, including Ms. Baumann. She let us talk and catch up for a long time before she had us sit down while she talked.

"Girls, for the next two months, we will be doing a community service project. We're going to go as a team every afternoon to the Faraway Community Center, where we're going to be teaching dance to underprivileged girls. Each one of you will be paired with a younger girl and will act as her mentor. In early March, we're going to help the girls put on a show for the entire community."

Ms. Baumann, who doesn't like to be interrupted, ignored some excited whispers and kept talking. "It will be your job to help the girls learn the dances so the show will be a big success."

Camilla, a senior and captain of the team, had been planning this with Ms. Baumann, and she stood up and talked about how this is the first time the dance team has ever done anything like this. "So it's up to all of us to make it work." When she said that, everyone cheered and nodded like we were all on board.

It's going to be a busy spring. Ms. Baumann told us that when the show is over, it's back to our regular rehearsal schedule so we'll be ready for the competitions we'll be doing in the spring and the state competition at the end of the school year. It all sounded great.

No complaints. For now.

7:42 p.m.

OK. Now I have something (or someone) to complain about. That someone is Brynn. She just called to ask if I have any ideas for the piece she's writing about Billy for the school paper. Seriously? I get that she likes him (even though she hasn't told me she does). But she knows I was upset when Billy and I broke up. Does she really think I want to help her come up with an idea for her article so she can gush about him? How about: "Student body president reunites with ex-girlfriend"?

Something tells me that's not the sort of article Brynn has in mind.

I don't like saying this, but I feel like I'm competing against my best friend for a boy we both like who happens to be our other best friend. And to make matters worse, Brynn seems to have figured out how she's going to get him.

She's going to write that article.

WHAT AM I GOING TO DO?

I know I made a resolution to get back together with Billy, but I don't know how I'm going to make that happen. I can't just call him up and say, "Hey, Billy, want to get back together?"

I might have made a resolution, but what I need is a plan.

Wednesday, 9:38 p.m.

Most mornings Dad drives me to school, but this morning I decided to walk. I thought it would be a good chance for me to think up a plan to get Billy back. I could hear Sophie saying, "*Thinking while walking is a very Zen thing to do.*" I was all set to walk and think and be Zen, but as I was coming out of my house, Matt Parker was coming out of his. "April, wait up. I'll walk with you."

My stomach flip-flopped as he crossed the yard between us. It's hard to look at him and not think how GORGEOUS he is. My mind flashed back to the time he saw me in my bikini trying to get a tan and nicknamed me California.

I took a breath and tried to compose myself. This was supposed to be the time I'd allocated to thinking about how I'm going to get back together with Billy, not walking to school and having Matt Parker flashbacks.

Matt smiled as he fell into place beside me. "I didn't know you walked to school."

"My dad usually drives me, but I felt like walking today."

"Cool!" Matt was still smiling. "The middle school is on my way."

The middle school *is* on the way to the high school, but I didn't want to be seen walking there with Matt Parker. For starters, just about everyone at Faraway Middle heard what had happened last semester with him. Plus, being seen with Matt didn't seem like such a good idea when my resolution is to get back together with Billy.

Matt was oblivious to my thoughts. "Practice for baseball season starts in February," he said. "I can't wait. I'm the starting first baseman." Matt smiled like he was proud.

"That's awesome." I was trying to focus on

what he was saying. "Starting as a ninth-grader, must be hard to do."

Matt nodded like he appreciated my recognition of his accomplishment. "You should come to one of my games." He grinned at me. It's hard not to notice how white his teeth are.

I was trying to decide if he said I should come because games are fun or if he had a bigger reason, like he'd like it if I saw him play. But as we got closer to the middle school, I stopped thinking about what might be going through Matt's brain and started thinking about what might be going through other people's, especially Billy's or Brynn's, if they saw us walking together.

I felt like I had to do something. I couldn't just walk by Faraway Middle with Matt Parker. As we got close to school, I put my backpack on the ground and started shuffling through it like I was looking for something.

Matt looked down at me. "Everything OK?" he asked.

I slapped my head. "I'm so dumb. I left my math assignment at home. I have to go back."

Matt glanced at his watch. "You better

hurry." Then he looked at me like he felt bad that I was in this predicament. We both knew he didn't have the time to go back with me and get to the high school.

"You go ahead." I waved and started to jog back in the other direction. I looked over my shoulder a few times until I saw Matt disappear around the corner. When he was out of sight, I stopped. Beads of sweat had formed on my forehead. I felt bad lying, especially since the truth is that I liked walking to school with Matt.

10:17 p.m.

OMG! Billy just FaceTimed me. He hasn't done that since we broke up, and I was totally NOT prepared for him to do it. My hair was in a ponytail and I was in my PJs, ready for bed. I debated whether I wanted to answer, but I did anyway.

"Why are you FaceTiming me so late?" I asked Billy when his face appeared on my screen. I was a little nervous it might be for a bad reason.

He smiled. "How's second semester going?"

I relaxed and started telling Billy about the

dance show at the community center and how I'll be working with a girl and teaching her to dance. As I talked, Billy scrunched up his forehead like he was thinking about something.

"What?" I asked.

"Do you think you could teach me to dance?" Billy asked.

I laughed. We both know he's a terrible dancer. "I don't know if that's possible."

Billy smiled into the phone. "I have moves that might surprise you, April."

"I hope I see them one day," I said.

Billy was still smiling as I hung up. He was teasing me like he used to when we went out.

A good sign, I think.

Friday, January 10, 10:04 p.m.
Text from Sophie

> Sophie: How are the newlyweds?
> Me: IDK
> Sophie: For real?
> Me: Fine. I guess.
> Me: Haven't seen them.

Sophie: Don't want to know why!
Me: Ewww!
Sophie: Ha ha! How are you?
Sophie: And Billy? Or Matt?
Sophie: Which is it?!?

I was trying to decide what to write back, and I couldn't. I didn't know how I wanted to answer the question. Ever since I walked to school with Matt, I've been thinking about him and why he asked me to come to one of his baseball games. But I've been thinking about Billy too. It was just like old times when he FaceTimed me, and it was fun. Is it even possible to like two guys at the same time? I literally started six different texts to Sophie and kept erasing what I'd written. Before I sent anything, Sophie texted me back.

Sophie: DWBH
Me: BFN

The second I pushed send, I regretted it. I'd wanted to write something that sounded as cool and effortless as "Don't worry, be happy," but "Bye for now" definitely fell short. I feel like such an idiot. Not just because this was the first time Sophie and I have texted and I *sounded* like an idiot, but because I'm thirteen, almost fourteen, and I can't even decide which boy I like.

It can't be normal to be that confused.

Can it?

Get your facts first, then you can distort them as much as you please.

—Mark Twain

Monday, January 13, 6:45 p.m.
On the couch

Today the dance team went to the Faraway Community Center and Ms. Baumann paired us up with the girls we're supposed to mentor. When we first got there, the girls were all over the place with their books, phones, and snacks. They were talking and laughing and definitely not what Ms. Baumann calls "dance ready." But it didn't take her long to get everyone in order. She was pairing girls with dancers faster than most people brush their teeth. When she brought a tiny ten-year-old girl over to me and introduced her as Desiree, I thought the girl might be scared or shy. She had to be smaller than June, who is only seven.

I gave her my best it's-going-to-be-okay smile. "I'm April," I said.

"You can call me Des." She put one hand on her hip and grinned. It was clear Des might be small, but her personality wasn't.

I sat down next to Des when Ms. Baumann started to talk. She told the girls we would be working with them for the next six weeks to help them prepare for a dance show they'll put on for the community. When she finished explaining the details, Ms. Baumann asked everyone to form three lines so we could begin rehearsal.

"There are two things you need to know before we start," Des said as we walked to a spot in the back line. I raised an eyebrow. She continued. "Number one: I love to talk."

Ms. Baumann clapped her hands. "Girls, take your places."

I put my fingers to my lips. Des bit hers to show she got that when Ms. Baumann is talking, no one else should be. Ms. Baumann explained a plié and then demonstrated how to do one. "Now it's your turn," she said.

Des just stood there. Her hand was back on her hip. I couldn't figure out what she was waiting for. "So what's the second thing?"

Des grinned like she was glad I'd asked. "I hate to dance."

Tuesday, January 14
Study Hall

This morning at assembly, Billy announced the upcoming student government activities, which include the school dance—on Friday, February 14. He did his best to try to get everybody excited.

"The dance is going to be better than ever this year because it falls on Valentine's Day," he said. Then he showed a really corny video he made of people dancing and kissing and having fun. When it was over, he promised there would be cool, never-before-seen-at-Faraway-Middle stuff at the dance. "I've been sworn to secrecy by the committee members," said Billy. "I can't divulge what we will have, but I can tell you that any lone females in need of a Valentine can count on me."

When he said that, a bunch of girls started clapping, cheering, and whistling. I thought Billy's offer sounded like a good thing too.

Until lunch. I was sitting with Brynn and Billy when Brynn said, "Hey Billy, I have the *perfect* angle for the newspaper article I want to write! Since the dance is going to be so awesome, I think it would be really interesting to everyone if I focus on what goes into planning it. What do you think?"

I froze. I thought I was going to choke on my chicken patty. I wanted to say I hated the idea, but I was scared if I did, it would have a reverse effect on Billy, the way that most things Mom says have on me.

Brynn kept talking. "I could shadow you while you go to planning meetings. I'll take notes and pictures, then my story could run the Monday after the dance. It'll be so cool for everyone to have an awesome time at the dance on Friday, then come to school Monday and read about what went into planning it." Brynn exhaled. "What do you think?"

I said a quick prayer. *Dear God, please let Billy hate that idea as much as I do.*

But apparently, I wasn't fast enough.

"I love it," said Billy. He put his hand up, and he and Brynn high-fived like we used to do in grade school, only then I used to like it. Billy kept talking. "The dance committee meetings are before school, so you'll have to get up early."

"I don't mind." Brynn's anything-for-the-story tone annoyed me.

Billy kept going. "Also, the meetings are closed-door. We don't want anyone to find out what we've got planned before the dance." He leaned across the table like what he was about to say next was for Brynn's ears only. "Will our secrets be safe with you?" he asked her.

Brynn leaned toward Billy. "Absolutely!"

Her you-can-trust-me voice was even more nauseating than her anything-for-the-story voice. I guess I should be grateful I didn't throw up chicken all over the cafeteria.

Wednesday, January 15, 10:02 a.m.
Science class

Ms. Thompson gave us a study hall this period, which I would use to study except I can't think about school when I can't stop thinking about what happened on the way to school. Ever since last week when Matt walked with me, I've been having Dad drive me. It's just that I made a resolution to try to get Billy back, so walking to school with Matt doesn't seem like a smart thing to do. But this morning, before I could leave the house with Dad, Matt actually knocked on our door and asked if I wanted to walk.

Grrr! I couldn't very well say no when he was standing right in front of me—plus he looked really cute in his hoodie and parka. So I walked to school with Matt, and here's the bad news (or the good news, depending on how you look at it, and I'm still not sure how I'm looking at it): I liked walking to school with him. He didn't talk about baseball this time. In fact, he didn't talk about himself at all. He wanted to talk about me, so I ended up telling him about the dance team going to the community center and the show we're helping with. I told him about Des and how she likes to talk and hates to dance. I even imitated how she talks with her hands on her hips.

When I finished the story, Matt laughed. "She sounds cute," he said.

I nodded. "She is." Then I looked around. We were standing right in front of the middle school. I'd been so absorbed in telling him my story, I didn't even realize it. I had no idea how long we'd been standing there or who might have seen us. I mean, SERIOUSLY? What is the point of standing in front of the middle school talking to a boy who has never liked me back when there's a boy in the middle school who used to like me and who I want to like me again?

Double grrr!

Study Hall, 1:33 p.m.
Stressed

At lunch, when Brynn and I got our trays, Billy was still in line, so we went ahead and sat down. Right when we got to the table, Brynn said, "I know a secret." I couldn't tell by her expression what it was about, but the only secret

I could think she might know was that she saw me walking to school this morning with Matt, and the only reason she wouldn't tell it is because she doesn't like to talk about him.

"You can tell me." I tried to stay calm. Brynn shook her head like I wasn't pulling any secrets out of her that easily. I eyed the line. Billy was almost through it. "Spill it," I said to Brynn. *And do it quickly.* I really didn't want her to say that she'd seen me walking to school with Matt in front of Billy.

That's when Brynn, whose back was to the cafeteria line, turned around like there was something she needed to see too. My stomach lurched. She and I both watched as Billy walked toward our table. I thought it was possible she was waiting for Billy to sit down with us before she announced that she'd seen me walking with Matt, but before he got there, she leaned across the table toward me. "The secret is that I went to my first dance committee planning meeting this morning, and trust me when I tell you . . . this dance is going to be awesoooome!" She rolled her eyes in Billy's direction and ran her fingers across her lips like that was all she could say for obvious reasons. Even though I don't like that she and Billy have secrets they can't share with me, I was glad it was all she had to say.

9:42 p.m.

Something good happened!

Billy called tonight to tell me a funny story about his Spanish teacher. "Señora Mendez got mad because Jake Willensky fell asleep on his desk during class. She snatched his book right out from under his head and threw it in the trash! He was so sound asleep that his head actually hit the desk." Billy laughed. "It was pretty funny."

"That's crazy!" I laughed.

"You mean *loco*," said Billy.

Then we both laughed. It felt so good to laugh with Billy again. It was just like old times. It made me completely un-confused and know for sure that I want to get back together with him. I can't believe I ever was confused. I can be such an idiot. I made a New Year's resolution to get back together with Billy—it's time to figure out a plan to do it.

The best laid plans
of mice and men often go awry.

—Robert Burns

Friday, January 17, 7:02 p.m.

Right when I got home from the community center, I called Billy to see if he wants to go on a bike ride tomorrow. I thought it was a genius plan. Apparently, I wasn't the only one who thought so, because Billy told me Brynn had already called him and that they're going on a bike ride tomorrow, but that I should definitely come too. So the three of us are going on a bike ride tomorrow. Not exactly what I had in mind.

Saturday, January 18, 9:42 a.m.
Deciding what to wear

It's so ridiculous that I can't decide what to wear on a bike ride I've been on dozens of times before, but I can't. I want to look cute. I need a fashion opinion. Easier said than done. I just asked Mom if she thought what I was wearing was good. All she said was that I need a heavier jacket because it's cold outside.

10:02 a.m.

I asked May and June what they thought about what I was wearing, and we had the most annoying conversation.

> Me: (in Converse and a baseball cap) May, do you like this outfit?
>
> May: Did you join a baseball team?
>
> Me: (changed into leggings and a fleece) June, do you think I look cute?
>
> June: Did you join a baseball team?

I gave up and put on the cap and Converse with the leggings and the fleece. I would have been better off asking the dog.

4:55 p.m.

Two words about today's bike ride: it sucked.

Brynn, Billy, and I did the same ride we've always done. We rode four miles to Rock Creek. When we got there, we stopped and took pictures of the three of us clowning around in the trees on the edge of the creek. After that, we pedaled west to Mr. Agee's farm, where we sat side by side on his fence and counted cows. Then we rode to 7-Eleven and bought Slurpees before heading home.

The problems started at Rock Creek. When we sat down on the bank of the creek to look at the pictures we'd taken, Brynn pulled up a picture on her phone of the three of us. "This is kind of crooked," she said. Then she started editing the photo, and when she straightened it, I got cropped out. "Look, this is cute," she said as she handed the phone to Billy.

I couldn't believe what she'd done. The same sort of thing happened when we got to Mr. Agee's farm. Brynn had packed water bottles for all of us. She's always been the one in charge of bringing drinks and snacks, and she's always brought three water bottles and three granola bars. But today she only had two of everything. "I can't believe I forgot to bring three," she said as she pulled the snacks and drinks from her bag. I thought she was going to say she forgot to bring one for me, but what she said was much worse. "Billy and I can share." Then she handed me a water and a granola bar like I was the odd man out.

And to be honest, I felt like it. We finished up the bike ride, but I wasn't into it. I didn't even have fun when we stopped to get Slurpees. It was so evident that Brynn likes Billy. She's being super aggressive about trying to get him. I guess it's also evident that if I want him back, I better do something about it too. ASAP!

Sunday, January 19, 5:02 p.m.
Confused.
Again.

This morning, I took May and June outside in the front yard to teach them how to rake pine needles into a house. Brynn and Billy and I used to love to make pine needle houses when we were little, and it made me kind of nostalgic thinking about it. Even though part of me is mad at Brynn for the way she's been acting lately, part of me misses her and the way we used to be.

Anyway, my sisters needed some convincing. "It's cold out here," said May.

"Yeah," said June. "It's cold out here."

I handed them each a rake. "You'll warm up when you start working." I showed them how to rake the pine needles into rooms with walls. "Leave an opening for a door there," I instructed June. As I was helping them, my mind wandered to Billy. When we used to make pine needle houses, he was the architect and he drew out intricate floor plans for Brynn and me to execute. I was picturing him as a third grader hunched over his drawing pad when I came up with a great idea. I decided to text Billy to see if he wanted to come over and help us make the house. It was a brilliant plan! May and June love Billy. They would be so excited if he helped us. I could picture how much fun we'd all have. I was composing the text on my phone when I realized I was suddenly engulfed in someone's shadow. I turned around.

Matt Parker was standing there. I shoved my phone with the unsent text into my pocket. He looked down at the ground around me. "Are you making pine needle houses?"

I didn't want to say that I was, but it was pretty obvious.

"Do you want to help us?" May asked.

I waited for him to say, *"I'll pass."* But he didn't. "Sure." Matt laughed. He took the rake from me and started raking. I watched speechlessly as he made a wall of pine needles.

"That's the kitchen," June said, pointing to the wall he was raking.

Matt nodded like it made perfect sense and kept raking.

I furrowed my brow as I watched him. He seemed oddly comfortable.

"Problem?" Matt asked like he was trying to read my thoughts.

I wasn't sure what to say. I didn't want to tell him that he had surprised me, in a good way. I wrapped my arms around my middle. "It's cold out here!" I said, like the temperature was my only issue.

Matt didn't miss a beat. He propped his rake against a tree, then put his arms around me and pulled me in next to him. I could feel his breath against my neck. "I'll warm you up," he said.

I was speechless. So were May and June. I could feel them both looking at me. Then May broke the silence. "Brynn!" she said, and waved. I turned my head in the direction May was waving. Even though Matt had made my heart start racing, I'm pretty sure it completely stopped when I saw Brynn.

She was standing there, open-mouthed. "I decided to walk over and see if you wanted to hang out," she said when I looked at her. Then she shrugged. "But I can see you're busy."

I thought Matt would let me go at that point, but he didn't.

Brynn gave Matt a disapproving look that seemed like it should be coming from my mother, not my best friend. "I'll come back another time," she said, and then turned and left.

I wanted to crawl under one of the piles of pine needles. I didn't like Brynn's reaction. I think Matt could tell I was upset. He squeezed me and then dropped his arms. “What’s her problem?” he asked.

I took a deep breath and shrugged. Not an answer I wanted to share with Matt Parker.

10:32 p.m.
Problems

I haven’t heard from Brynn all day, and I can’t decide if I should call her.

I know if I try to explain that what she saw isn’t what she thinks she saw, she’ll say it couldn’t possibly be anything else. She has probably already called Billy and told him what happened. Unfortunately, that’s not even my biggest problem.

My biggest problem is that I’ve been confused all day. It’s what happens whenever I’m around Matt Parker. He’s the only thing that has ever come between Billy and me (well, except for Brynn), and I’m not going to let that happen again. What’s the point?! He doesn’t *like* me, like me. He likes to flirt with me, or rake with me, or walk with me. But that’s it. I’m done being confused about Matt Parker. He’s gorgeous and mysterious and my neighbor, but that's it. I LIKE BILLY!

What I need to be thinking about is Billy and how to get him back.

It can't be that hard. It would be nice if I had someone to talk with about this, like a best friend. But I don't! My best friend is off doing what I should be doing, which is getting the boy of her dreams. How is she doing it? By giving him gifts and writing an article about him and sharing water bottles and granola bars. I wouldn't have called that a perfect plan, but it seems to be working better than anything I've come up with.

And now she can tell Billy that she saw me in my front yard hugging Matt Parker. If Billy didn't like her before, he will now. Brynn should thank me for practically handing her Billy.

How could I be so stupid to let Matt hug me in full view of the neighborhood? If I hadn't gotten four As and one B on my last report card, I'd be seriously concerned for my intelligence. Now putting my brain to work on a brilliant plan of my own. I just don't know what it is yet.

10:47 p.m.
Online

According to Google results, the top ten ways to get your boyfriend back are as follows:

1. Give him space.
2. Play hard to get.
3. Kill him with kindness.
4. Dress more attractively.
5. Hang out where he does.
6. Be irresistible.
7. Find a new hobby.
8. Focus more on school or work.
9. Laugh when he talks.
10. Stand up straight.

Just one question: when the Internet makes me more confused than ever, how am I supposed to figure out what to do?

There is no greater agony than bearing an untold story inside you.

—Maya Angelou

Wednesday, January 22, 6:17 p.m.

I've been trying very hard for the last few days NOT to think about the Billy situation, and the reason for that is because I have NO idea what I think about it, or more specifically, what to do about it. I've been racking my brain trying to come up with a plan, but I haven't come up with anything. It's put me in a rotten mood all week, which was the mood I was in when I got to the community center this afternoon.

"What's wrong with you, Miss Grumpy

Pants?" Des asked as we started rehearsal.

"Nothing," I lied. I replicated the jazz step Ms. Baumann had just demonstrated. "Your turn," I said to Des. She shook her head and planted her feet on the floor.

"C'mon!" I tried to coax her into moving. "You need to learn the step."

Des's hands were on her hips. "I'll do the step when you tell me what's wrong."

I let out a loud breath. For a cute little kid, she could be very frustrating. I wasn't going to tell her about my boy problems, but the next thing I knew, Ms. Baumann was pointing to me like I'd better get my student moving. "Just tell me what it's about," whispered Des. "Then I'll dance."

"Fine," I said. "Boy issues."

Ms. Baumann gave us both a stern look as Des let out a whoop. Thankfully, she did the step. "I love boy issues," said Des.

This was ridiculous. "What do you know about boys? You're ten."

Des's grin was as big as her face. "I know a lot. I watch TV." Des was serious. "Go ahead.

Tell me your problem, and I'll tell you how to solve it."

I pointed to Ms. Baumann, who was demonstrating the next step in the dance. "Go!" I said when Ms. Baumann told the girls to try it.

Des shook her head at me. "You first."

I groaned. It was impossible to reason with her. I knew I'd have to talk if I wanted her to dance. "My problem is that I had a boyfriend, we broke up, and now I want him back."

"Easy," said Des. "Go get him."

I shook my head at her. "That's not how it works."

"Then tell me how it works." Her feet were glued to the floor. It was clear she wasn't going anywhere.

"Boys can be complicated," I said.

"Not as complicated as learning to dance," she said. Des sat down on the floor and gave me her I'd-rather-talk-than-dance look. I'm not sure which will be more complicated—finding a way to get back together with Billy or teaching her to dance.

Thursday, January 23, 1:33 p.m.
Study Hall

Mr. Barton just told Brynn and me that if we can't stop laughing, he's sending us to the office. Unfortunately, it's not so easy to stop laughing after what happened at lunch.

As Brynn and I were leaving the cafeteria, the most jaw-dropping thing happened. Brynn pointed to Ashley Simon, who was coming out of the bathroom. Ashley's skirt was tucked into the back of her underwear, and you could see the letters THUR written across her butt.

"Isn't she a little old to be wearing days-of-the-week panties?" I asked.

Apparently, I wasn't the only one who thought so, because laughter spread as Ashley walked through the cafeteria. When she passed Kelly Blake, Kelly stopped her and whispered in her ear. There was clapping and whistling as Ashley pulled her skirt out of her underwear and ran out of the cafeteria.

Brynn and I cracked up. "She had it coming to her," said Brynn. She looped a conspiratorial arm around me. "Justice is served!"

I knew we were both thinking about the time Ashley "accidentally" spilled a carton of milk on me in fourth grade, which made it look like I'd wet my pants. Brynn told the teacher that Ashley had done it on purpose, but it was her word against Ashley's, and Ashley managed to escape trouble. To this day, it bothers Brynn. She can be such a good friend.

I just wish it happened more often.

Friday, January 24, 1:48 p.m.
Study Hall
Ultra annoyed

At lunch today, Billy had to make up a test, so it was just Brynn and me. All she could talk about was how awesome the Valentine's dance is going to be. "The committee is making such amazing plans," she said, like it was a big, exciting secret.

I nodded like I appreciated she'd told me that, even though I didn't because I knew she was going to say she couldn't tell me more. Brynn continued. "I never knew how much work went into planning these things. It's been really special to get to watch it happen."

"I'm sure," I said unenthusiastically.

Brynn eyed me like she was trying to interpret my response. "I'm sure it's hard for you to understand," she said. "I wish I could tell you all the cool stuff that's in the works. But when you see it, you'll get what I'm talking about." Then Brynn looked at me like she felt sorry for me.

I felt sorry for me too . . . I had to sit there listening to her!

10:33 p.m.

Starting to bore myself

My brain is literally consumed with the Billy/Brynn situation. I feel like Brynn and I are just pretending to be friends, and I have no idea how to get Billy back. I know I've overthought the whole thing, and now it's like I'm paralyzed and can't do anything.

Tonight I really needed someone to talk to, so I called Sophie. I wasn't even sure she would answer, but she picked up on the first ring like she was super happy to hear from me.

I told her about the sweater and the bike ride

and the picture and the secrets about the dance that Billy and Brynn *can't* tell me.

"I know Brynn likes him. I hate that she won't tell me she does, but it sucks even more that we're supposed to be best friends, or we were, and now we're really not." I let out a breath. "I like Billy, but I don't know how to tell him I do. It's all so complicated."

Sophie was quiet for a while, like she was thinking. "It's really not complicated," she said. "It sounds like a lot of the stuff you're describing falls into the things-that-don't-matter category."

"They matter to me," I said defensively.

"I didn't mean they don't matter," Sophie said, like she hadn't meant to be hurtful. "I just meant it's small stuff and you should let it go." I was quiet, so she continued. "Talk to Brynn and Billy. Just be honest." Sophie made everything sound so simple. And it probably would be.

For her.

Sunday, January 26, 7:02 p.m.
Home from the diner

Today Dad's brother, Uncle Marty, and his

son, Sam, drove in from Mobile. It was Sam's birthday, so Dad closed the Love Doctor Diner early and we all had dinner together. We don't see Uncle Marty and Sam very often, but when we do, it's always interesting. Like tonight. It started when Dad asked Sam how he was doing. "I just turned five." He held up four fingers.

Uncle Marty smiled at Sam. "He hasn't quite gotten the counting thing down yet."

"When I poop, I can wipe myself," said Sam. May and June looked at each other and started laughing. I have to admit, I thought it was pretty funny too. Even Mom couldn't help smiling.

"Sam, remember what we talked about," said Uncle Marty. "That's not table talk."

Sam didn't seem to remember. "Dad wipes himself when he poops too. I've seen him do it," said Sam.

"Sam!" said Uncle Marty. May and June were falling out of their chairs. I was laughing too. But Sam was just getting started. "When I eat corn you can see it in my poop." Sam pulled his khaki pants away from his belly and stuck his hand down them. I don't know what he was looking for. Maybe poop with corn in it. I was laughing so hard, tears were rolling down my cheeks. May and June were literally on the floor.

"Girls, that's enough," said Mom. She made everybody sit back down and gave Uncle Marty a look like he needed to do something to restore some order.

He pulled Sam's hand out of his pants. "Sam, why don't you tell everyone about Cassie."

Sam nodded like he was happy to talk about her. "We're getting married. I got a ring in the gumball machine at the car wash, and tomorrow on the playground I'm going to ask her to marry me." I bit my lip. I knew I shouldn't laugh.

Sam pulled the ring out of his pocket and showed it to us.

I could tell Uncle Marty thought it was cute. "Sam, tell them why you think Cassie is going to say yes when you ask her to marry you."

Sam sat up straight while he talked. It was easy to see his confidence on this topic. "Cassie is going to say yes when I ask her to marry me because the other day at lunch, she gave me one of her Oreos."

His answer made me smile. Love sure is simple when you're five. I wish it was that easy at thirteen.

That's one small step for man, one giant leap for mankind.

—Neil Armstrong

Tuesday, January 28, 7:02 p.m.

I'm a genius.

I think.

We had a day off from practice at the community center, so I decided to ask Billy to come over to help me find good music to download. It was a last-minute idea, and Billy said yes, so I decided to take it as a sign that today was the day I should do the Sophie thing and just be honest and tell him how I feel. But it was kind of hard to do when he first got to my house because when May and June saw him, they went nuts.

"Billy!" screamed May.

"Billy!" screamed June.

They were all over him, and both made him give them piggyback rides down the hall. When they finally left us alone, we sat down on the floor of my room to listen to music. "Do you still like Coldplay?" Billy asked.

I bumped my shoulder into his. "You know I'll always love Coldplay." Billy reached down and took over my laptop. "We Never Change" started to play. It's not their most popular song, but it's really pretty. Billy and I sat side by side, listening. Neither of us said anything as we listened, but the meaning of the lyrics wasn't lost on me. I couldn't help but think that Billy had chosen that song for a reason. As the music played, I let my knee fall so that it was touching his. He didn't move his knee away, but he didn't move it closer either. I looked at Billy, but I couldn't read his expression.

"What are you thinking?" he asked when the song ended.

It was my chance to say something, the perfect moment to tell Billy how I feel. As he looked at me, I thought maybe he was waiting for me to say something about us, about everything that happened. I opened my mouth to speak, but the words stuck in my throat. I wanted to say just the right thing, and suddenly I didn't know what that thing was.

I think Billy sensed my hesitation. "Want to listen to another song?" he asked. Before I could answer, Justin Timberlake's voice filled my room. The perfect moment passed almost as quickly as it had presented itself. Billy and I sat on my floor listening to music until his mom called and told him he had to come home for dinner.

Part of me is upset. I mean, I blew it. At least, I think I did. Another part of me feels like maybe I didn't. This was the first time in a long time that Billy and I were how we used to be. Just April and Billy. That's a step in the right direction.

Isn't it?

Wednesday, January 29, 6:15 p.m.
Home from the community center

"So how are things with you and B-man?" Des asked while we were going over the steps of the hip-hop dance she's going to be doing at the show.

"B-man?" I asked, even though I knew she meant Billy. My boy drama had become her favorite distraction. "We need to focus on your dancing, not my love life."

Des ignored what I'd said. "Are things good?"

"Yep." I nodded, then did a series of moves. "Your turn."

Des copied what I'd done. It didn't exactly look like what I'd done, but at least she tried. "Define good," said Des.

We'd developed a pattern. I talked. Then she danced.

"Billy came over, and we hung out and listened to music," I said.

Des wrinkled her nose like something smelled funny. "How's that good?"

I shook my head like I didn't want to get further into this, but Des clearly did. "If you're trying to get Billy back, I don't see how hanging out and listening to music counts as good. You could do that with anybody. Your dad. Your grandma. Even your dog."

I'd basically had the same thought, but I didn't like hearing it from Des. "I'm not going to sit here explaining the subtleties of a relationship to you."

She shook her head. "It doesn't sound like a relationship."

I flinched. Des could tell she'd hit a nerve. "You just need to look for a sign that he likes you," she added.

"Right," I said. But I felt pretty stupid taking relationship advice from a ten-year-old.

10:02 p.m.

Billy just texted me. Two words: Sweet dreams.

I'm taking it as a sign.

Friday, January 31, 10:44 p.m.

Rotten Day

It's confirmed: the world is against me. As of last night, everything was great. Billy called me before I went to bed, and we talked for forty-three minutes. When we hung up, his last words to me were, "I miss this."

"Me too," I said softly. It was perfect.

But between the time I hung up with Billy last night and the time I got to school this morning, everything had gone wrong. I know I shouldn't blame other people for my problems, but what happened this morning was Dad's fault.

I've been getting a ride to school from him every day, so I haven't had to walk with Matt and take a chance of people seeing me with him. But today, Dad left early without even telling me, so I had no choice but to walk. When I went outside, Matt was standing in his yard like he was waiting for me.

"I'm glad you're walking today," he said. "I've been wanting to talk to you." I couldn't imagine why Matt Parker wanted to talk to me. He motioned to his own house. "Has anyone come to your house asking who lives next door?"

He was making no sense. "Why would someone do that?"

Matt didn't really say. He just kept asking if anyone had come to our house asking about who lives in the neighborhood or if I'd seen any strangers hanging out on our street. I couldn't figure out where any of it was coming from. He was weirdly intense. I tried to lighten the mood. "Are you expecting a talent scout?"

Matt half-smiled, like he somewhat appreciated my attempt at humor. As we walked toward Faraway Middle, I kept asking why he was asking me such strange questions until he pointed and said, "Isn't that your friend Brynn?"

I froze. Brynn was standing there with a book open like she was reading, but that wasn't what she was doing, because when Matt pointed to her, I saw her look down. By the time I'd walked into the gates, Brynn was gone, but she'd seen us. It shouldn't matter that I was walking with Matt, but I knew it did. I decided to say something to Brynn, but she beat me to it. After morning assembly, Brynn came up to me.

"I saw you this morning." It was her way of saying she saw me with Matt and didn't approve.

"We just walked to school together," I said. "It's nothing."

"First in your front yard. Now, walking to school." Brynn shrugged. "It doesn't seem like nothing."

It was the first time Brynn had brought up the front yard sighting. I'd been hoping she wouldn't, that it would somehow magically have disappeared from her memory bank, but clearly it hadn't. Now I felt like I had to defend myself. "He's my next-door neighbor," I said, like that explained everything.

Brynn looked at me in this weird, blank way. "Hmmm," she said.

I wasn't completely sure what *"Hmmm"* meant. I took it to mean, *"I can't wait to tell Billy what I just saw."* I'm not certain she had told Billy when she saw Matt and me in my front yard, but now I'm pretty sure she's told him about both sightings, because she and Billy weren't in the cafeteria at lunch, and I didn't see Billy for the rest of the day. I was hoping that he would call tonight or at least text. But he didn't.

Not a good sign.

True friends stab you in the front.

—*Oscar Wilde*

Saturday, February 1, 9:42 a.m.
Problems

I just called Billy to see if he wanted to hang out today, and I'm pretty sure by his reaction that things between us have changed. He said, "Student government is getting together to make posters for the dance. I have to go. I'm late." His tone was informational. He didn't sound like the Billy who had called two nights earlier and said, "*I miss this.*" The only reason I could think of that his attitude had changed was because Brynn told him about seeing me with Matt, and he's pissed.

When I hung up with him, I called Brynn to see if she wanted to hang out. I wanted to see if I could get out of her what she'd said to Billy. But she didn't want to hang out. "I'm getting together with the student government dance committee to help make posters," she told me.

"I thought you were just observing what they do and writing an article about it," I said.

"That's all it was supposed to be," said Brynn. "But I've been spending so much time with them, they made me an honorary member of the committee."

CRAP.

4:38 p.m.
Weirded out
In more ways than one

I'm sure Brynn told Billy about seeing me with Matt. I get why she would. If she likes Billy (which clearly she does), she knows how sensitive Billy is about the subject of Matt and me. She knows that if he heard I was hanging out with Matt, there's no chance Billy would like me. But here's what doesn't quite add up:

It's not like Billy and I act flirty when we're together, especially around Brynn, so she doesn't have a reason to think he likes me and not her. Unless she's just worried about the fact that he used to like me.

Or maybe she does have a reason. Maybe she knows Billy doesn't realize how she feels about him because he's told her how he feels about me. But I don't think Billy would do that. Plus, I'm not even sure how he feels about me.

I actually spent a big chunk of this morning looking in Mom's magnifying mirror, counting my pores and trying to imagine what those two must have been saying about me. The more I thought about it, the more my thoughts began to swirl around in a giant circle that didn't lead down a path toward any answers.

It had me a little weirded out, so after lunch, I decided to take Gilligan on a walk. Surprise, surprise—when I did, I saw Matt. "Want to hang out?" he asked.

"Sure," I said. Since all my other friends were off together making posters and, in all likelihood, talking about me, I didn't see that it made much difference. So I went over to Matt's, and we sat on his couch and watched TV. For a Saturday, it was strangely quiet at his house. "Where are your parents?" I asked.

"My mom is at work," Matt said. He didn't mention his dad. Then he looked at me. "I really don't want to talk."

Did that mean he wanted to kiss? That's all I could figure. And even though the only thing I've been thinking about lately is getting back together with Billy, as I sat there beside Matt on the couch and thought about Brynn talking to Billy about me and Billy barely speaking to me this morning, what I was thinking was that I wanted to kiss Matt too. I moved a little closer to him and tilted my face toward his. It seemed like the perfect moment.

Matt looked at me. Then he looked down. "You should probably get going," he said. "I have baseball practice this afternoon."

It wasn't what I'd expected him to say. I felt like such an idiot. The next thing I knew, I was walking home with Gilligan and a head full of even worse thoughts than I'd gone there with.

The whole day was so weird. Sometimes it seems like Matt likes me, and then he has a chance to kiss me, but doesn't. It's so hard to figure him out.

He's like a Rubik's Cube. Nothing ever lines up perfectly.

Does he like me? Or doesn't he? How does Billy feel? Did Brynn tell him what she saw? Does Billy still feel the way he did the other night when we talked? Was he really in a hurry to go this morning because he was late?

Way too many questions. Not enough answers.

Monday, February 3, 1:39 p.m.
Study Hall

This morning, the school dance was the only thing anyone was talking about. When I got to school, there were posters up everywhere. There was a student government rep stationed at every poster passing out teaser pins that said, *What will happen at the dance?*

Brynn had her camera around her neck, and she was following Billy everywhere, snapping pictures and making notes on her phone. When Billy saw me, he did this weird half-wave. I couldn't tell if it meant "I'm too busy being president to stop and talk" or "I'm pissed."

"Isn't this cool?" Brynn said when she passed me in the hall.

"Yeah," I lied.

Friday, February 7, 9:45 p.m.
Back to normal

Until this afternoon, I would've classified this as a mostly uneventful week of unsuccessful attempts to a) teach Des to dance, b) figure out if Billy still feels the same way he did when he said, "*I miss this*," and c) forget about Matt saying, "You should probably get going." Then something eventful happened.

Brynn called and asked if I wanted to go shopping tomorrow for dresses to wear to the dance. "It's been way too long since we've done something fun together," she said. Then she went on for a long time about how much fun we always have when we shop together—which we do, it's true. So I said yes, and as we talked about where we were going to go and what we were going to buy and when we would meet, it felt like everything was normal again.

10:02 p.m.
Back to NOT

I thought about it more, and just because Brynn asked me to go shopping with her doesn't mean her feelings about Billy have changed. For all I know, she wants me to go shopping with her because she knows I trust her taste in clothes. How do I know she's not just trying to get me to buy a dress that looks terrible on me? What was I thinking? Things aren't normal at all!

10:32 p.m.

Sophie just called, and I thought maybe it was because she has some kind of Zen ESP thing and could sense that I needed to talk, but that wasn't it. "If you had to choose between cinnamon or sage, which color would you pick?"

"Aren't those spices?"

"Irrelevant," said Sophie. "It's for a project I'm working on. Don't think, just pick."

"Cinnamon," I said.

Sophie exhaled like I'd given her the answer she was looking for. "So, how are you?" she asked. I gave a rundown of everything that's happened since the last time we talked. I told her about Billy calling and saying, *"I miss this,"* and Brynn seeing me with Matt and possibly telling Billy, and hanging out at Matt's, and then about Brynn asking me to go shopping. "How do I know she'd not going to convince me to buy a dress that looks terrible on me?"

"Wow," she said when I finished. "One thing at a time. First, I thought you were going to tell Billy how you feel."

I groaned into the phone. "I was going to. But I can't now. I don't know what Brynn told him, so I don't know how he feels about me. I don't want to tell him I like him and then have him say he doesn't like me."

Sophie made an *ehhh* sound, like she didn't quite agree with my reasoning. "OK, what about Brynn? Why don't you tell her when you go shopping that you still like Billy and that it bothers you that you think she likes Billy, and you don't like how it's affecting your friendship."

"I can't."

"Why not?" asked Sophie.

"What would I say? He was my boyfriend first, and I don't like that you gave him a nice gift and that you're writing an article about him so you can spend time with him?"

"Something like that," said Sophie.

"Brynn and I are best friends. We should be able to talk about anything, but we can't."

I waited for Sophie to agree. I thought she was going to say something prophetic about how friendships change and it's hard when they do, but she didn't.

"Why don't you acknowledge how you really feel?" Sophie spoke slowly and quietly, like she wanted to make sure her words sank in. "I think you should admit that you don't want Brynn to have Billy, but you don't really want him for yourself. Maybe you want him to always be there for you, but I think the one you want to be with is Matt."

"No!" I'd just told Sophie how upset I was about Brynn possibly telling Billy she saw me with Matt and how that messes up all my plans (not that I had any good ones) to get back together with Billy. "I don't get why you would say that," I said to Sophie.

She laughed into the phone like I was the one who wasn't getting it. "Because it's the truth."

I'm the girl who—I call it girl-next-door-itis—the hot guy is friends with . . . but never considers dating.

—Taylor Swift

Saturday, February 8, 6:45 p.m.

Brynn and I went to the mall this morning. When we first got there, I wasn't sure how the day was going to turn out. Brynn was totally focused on finding her dress first. Once we did, she wanted to look for shoes to go with it. We went into three different stores before she finally settled on a pair of black wedges. But after that, she was totally into helping me. "April, check this out," she said when we went into a small boutique with cool stuff. She was holding up a pink beaded mini dress. "It's super cute, your size, and on sale."

When she showed it to me, the first thing I thought was that it might be too glam. The dress she'd just gotten was all black and much simpler. The thought that Brynn wouldn't give me good fashion advice flashed through my head again. I could picture everyone staring at me and whispering as I showed up in a way-too-glitzy dress.

"You don't think it's too much for a school dance, do you?"

Brynn put the dress in my hands. "Just try it on."

When I did, I couldn't help but smile. It fit perfectly, and the price was right. "It's awesome," I said to Brynn.

She squealed. "I told you!" After we got the dress, we found some gold flats to go with it, and then we went to the food court to get lunch. I thought about Sophie's advice to be honest. I figured it was a good chance to at least try and talk to her about things. "This was fun," I said as we sat down with our salads.

"Yeah," Brynn said. I knew she got what I meant.

"I feel like we've gotten kind of far apart

lately, and it bums me out." I tried to say it lightly. I didn't want it to seem like I was making too big a deal out of things.

Brynn nodded like she agreed. "I know. It's been hard. I've been so busy with the dance and the story for the paper." She shrugged like that explained it, but it didn't.

"So who do you want to dance with at the dance?" I tried to ask in a sing-songy kind of way, like I wasn't concerned about anyone in particular.

Brynn took a bite of her salad. "No one special," she said after she swallowed.

I looked at her to see if she was telling the truth. But her face didn't give away anything. There were still a lot of things I wanted to ask her, like why she brought me back a T-shirt from her ski trip and Billy a sweater, and if she likes him as more than a friend, and if she told Billy that she saw me with Matt. But she stood up and dumped the rest of her barely eaten salad in the trash, and I knew I couldn't ask those things. She wouldn't have answered anyway.

Conversation over. It was the most I was going to get from Brynn.

Sunday, February 9, 10:42 p.m.
A text from Billy

Billy: What's up?
Me: Not much.
Me: You?
Billy: Not much.

I waited to see what else he would write, but it didn't seem like he was going to, so I did.

Me: Going to bed.
Billy: Yeah. Me too.
Me: Nighty night.
Billy: :-)

His text didn't exactly say *I want to get back together*, but it also didn't say *Brynn told me she saw you with Matt, and I'm pissed.* All in all, a pretty good text.

Monday, February 10, 1:34 p.m.
Study Hall

The only thing anyone at school is talking

about is the dance on Friday night. In PE, Julia Lozano told everyone she heard there's going to be a real DJ. After assembly, Jake Willensky told everyone he heard there was going to be a Dippin' Dots cart. At lunch, Billy was at a dance committee meeting and Brynn was in the newsroom editing what she said will be "the best piece ever" in the *Faraway Middle News*, so I sat with Emily, Kate, and Vanessa, and they were talking about the dance too. "I heard there's going to be a dance contest," Emily said.

"With awesome prizes," Kate added.

Vanessa grinned. "Put my name on one!" She smiled with confidence.

I felt the excitement too. Hopefully, we hadn't been going to dance practice every day since school started for nothing. As I was listening to Emily talk about what we should do to win the contest, my mind was picturing Billy watching me dance in my pink dress. And that's when it hit me. At the dance, I'm going to tell Billy I want to get back together. It'll be perfect timing. I can't believe I didn't think of it before.

"Earth to April," I heard Emily say as I was

picturing Billy and me happily slow dancing to the last song of the night.

I looked up, startled. "Oops, sorry!" I said. But the only thing I was really sorry about was that it had taken me so long to think up this brilliant plan.

Wednesday, February 12, 9:45 p.m.
Deep in thought

I spent most of today thinking about talking to Billy at the dance. Even though he hasn't said anything else to me about how he feels, he did text me the other night, and I could tell from his text that he's not mad. I think I just need to do what Sophie said and tell him how I feel. And what better time to do it than at the Valentine's Day dance, when I'll be wearing my new pink, sparkly dress? The more I thought about it, the more excited I was.

It was what I was thinking about when I got to the community center after school. Des took one look at me and said, "Why are you all smiles today?"

Usually I make Des dance before I give her

any info, but today I didn't. I launched right into my plan to tell Billy that I want to get back together. When I finished talking, Des frowned. "I don't like it," she said.

I was sure she would. "You're the one who told me to 'go get him.'"

She shook her head. "I didn't mean like that."

"Then how?" I asked.

"I don't know," Des said slowly, like she was actually putting a lot of thought into what I was going to do. "It just seems weird to show up at a dance and tell your old boyfriend that you want to get back together. It's, like, too planned."

I let out a deep breath. Then Ms. Baumann said it was time to dance. For a minute, what Des said bothered me. But as we started to go over the hip-hop steps, I decided to let her ten-year-old nonsense go. I don't even know why I told her what I'm doing anyway.

Thursday, February 13, 9:45 p.m.
Off the phone

Billy just called. We didn't talk for long, but I'm glad he called.

"Tomorrow is going to be a busy day with the dance and everything, so before things get crazy, I just wanted to say hi."

"Hi," I said in a flirty voice.

Billy laughed. "Hi," he said back.

We both laughed. Any worries I still had about Brynn having said something to him about seeing me with Matt or him being mad melted away. "So, do you think the dance will be fun?" I asked.

"I do," said Billy. "Especially for some people."

"What do you mean by that?" I had to ask.

Billy stalled, like he was thinking. "I just meant there are lots of surprises in store."

That's when it hit me. What if Billy is planning to do the same thing at the dance that I'm planning to do? What if one of the surprises he's talking about is that he's going to tell me he wants to get back together? We've definitely had some good moments lately. Billy doesn't say things unless he means them. Visions of me in sparkly pink, dancing with him, float through my head.

I officially can't wait until tomorrow!

It is difficult to know
at what moment love begins;
It is less difficult to know
that it has begun.

—Henry Wadsworth Longfellow

Friday, February 14, 7:32 a.m.

Happy Valentine's Day!

This morning I washed and flat-ironed my hair, put on my new red-and-white-striped sweater, white jeans, and pink lip gloss, and gave May and June boxes of candy hearts, which I convinced Mom to let them eat at breakfast. "You're the best big sister ever," May said as she ate her hearts without even bothering to read the messages on them.

"Yeah," June said, like she genuinely agreed and wasn't just repeating what she'd heard.

"You're the best big sister ever." She read each message out loud before she popped the hearts in her mouth. *Crazy for you. Soul mate. Wink wink.* The words sounded funny coming out of her seven-year-old mouth, and everyone laughed as she read them.

I don't have much time to write. Dad's about to drive me to school. I just took a deep Sophie-style breath and let out a big sigh of happy air. The day is off to an excellent start!

1:38 p.m.
Study Hall

This day has continued to go shockingly well. This morning, all of my teachers let us have Valentine's celebrations in class. Mrs. Thompson even brought in pink glazed doughnuts and gave each of us cards that said *You light my Bunsen burner.* It was weird—and maybe slightly inappropriate—but still, it was sweet of her to try.

At lunch, Brynn was in the newsroom putting the "finishing touches" on her article, which meant I got to eat lunch alone with Billy. "So, are you ready for the dance tonight?" he asked.

He bumped my shoulder with his like we used to do when we were going out.

I nodded. "Want to tell me about any of the surprises you have planned?" I looked right into Billy's eyes as I spoke.

Billy held my gaze. "That's for me to know and you to find out."

I can't wait to find out!

5:30 p.m.
Home from the community center

Being anxious about tonight because of a card is dumb.

I'd been excited all day about the dance tonight and the possibility of what might happen with Billy, but something happened at the community center that dampened my spirits. There was no rehearsal this afternoon, just a party. Ms. Baumann brought juice and heart-shaped cookies with red and white sprinkles. Everyone on the dance team gave the girls at the community center cards we'd made. The one I'd made for Des had a lip kiss on the front that I'd done myself with Mom's red lipstick.

Des had made a card for me too. She'd drawn a picture of a sandwich and a bag of potato chips on the front. I thought it was a strange image for a Valentine's card. "*I hope you get the sandwich and the chips*," it said on the inside. I shook my head at Des. "I don't mean to be dumb, but I'm not sure I get it."

She shrugged. "I hope you get everything you want tonight," she said. Then she lowered her voice. "You know, like, if it doesn't work out, I don't want you to be disappointed."

I felt my stomach turn over. As I sat there munching cookies and sipping juice, I found myself wondering if her words were in some way weirdly prophetic. I thought about it all the way home. Bottom line: it's stupid to worry about a strange Valentine's card when I have a dance to get ready for.

6:43 p.m.
Dressed
But not sure I'm ready

Not that May and June are fashion experts, but when they saw me dressed for the dance, they both said, "You look pretty!" at the same time. They were a chorus of sameness, which usually bothers me, but tonight I liked it.

Mom called Dad to come home from the diner so he could take pictures. "You look beautiful, sweetheart," he said when he saw me.

Even though he's my dad, it was nice to hear it. I just hope Billy has the same reaction. Hopefully when he sees me, he'll know for sure (I mean, hopefully he knows already) that he wants to get back together. I was so confident about it the other night when we were on the phone, but now I'm not so sure. Des's card kind of weirded me out. If he doesn't say something to me, I can still say something to him. That was my original plan anyway.

Not a big deal. Either way, tonight should have a happy ending.

11:17 p.m.

Happy endings don't exist
At least, not at school dances

Tonight was the most disastrous night ever.

It didn't start that way. The gym looked

amazing. There were silver sparkly things hanging from the ceiling, lights everywhere, a DJ, a crepe maker, and a Dippin' Dots cart. When I walked in, I could tell everyone was super pumped and upbeat. Brynn was already there talking to Heather, Kelly, and Julia. I walked up to their group, and Brynn gave me a huge hug. "You look gorgeous!" she squealed.

"I love your dress!" Heather said. Kelly and Julia both nodded in agreement.

"See!" Brynn said. "Aren't you glad I made you get it?"

I was. It actually made me feel a little bad that I had doubted Brynn. I looked around for Billy, who was talking to the DJ. Brynn must have followed my gaze to where he was standing. "Official business," she said. The way she said it was a little weird, like she was his assistant or something, but I decided it was something that fell into Sophie's *little stuff* category so I let it go.

I was glad I did. When Billy finished what he was doing, he walked over to where we were all talking. "Look at you!" he said. He was smiling.

I smiled back. I could feel myself starting to relax into the night.

When the music started, everyone danced. The DJ was amazing, and when the dance contest started, Emily, Kate, Vanessa and I all gravitated to the middle of the gym. The dance floor was packed, and everyone was going crazy during the contest.

"Give it up for the winners!" the DJ finally boomed. The four of us plus Ian Sanders and Jack Hewitt won. It was awesome. Everyone clapped and cheered as the DJ gave each of us gift certificates for two free movie tickets.

The night had been really fun up to this point. I was happily picturing myself at the movies, holding hands with Billy. Even though Billy hadn't said anything to me yet about wanting to get back together, I wasn't worried. There hadn't been an opportunity, and as student government president, he was busy making sure everything was going OK. So when the DJ put on a slow song and announced that it was time for the final dance, I knew it was time to put my plan into action. I looked around the gym for Billy. I wanted to find him and ask him to dance. It was the perfect time to tell him that I want to get back together.

But when I looked across the gym and found Billy, he was already dancing.

With Brynn!

My stomach lurched. I didn't want it to be obvious that I was watching them. I didn't want to watch them, but my eyes were glued to their every move. What I saw was so totally not what I was expecting. It was like a nightmare I couldn't wake up from. Billy had his hands around Brynn's waist. She leaned into him and pressed her boobs against his chest. Billy smiled. His hands dropped lower on her waist. Then, Brynn smiled at Billy and kissed him on the cheek. I watched her lips linger for a few seconds. They looked at each other as they danced, and that's when it hit me: they're already a couple. My plan to get back together with Billy wasn't happening. Before the song even ended, I went outside and texted Dad to come pick me up.

I'd seen enough for one night.

11:59 p.m.
More than upset

I can't sleep. I just can't believe what happened tonight. I was so sure Billy felt the same way I did. I never dreamed that the girl he likes is Brynn. My best friends are a couple. I can't even believe I just wrote that. The way I'd imagined the night turning out and the way it actually did had absolutely nothing in common. I think about what Des wrote in her card and what she said to me this afternoon at the community center. My worst fears have been confirmed. Brynn likes Billy. Billy likes Brynn.

End of the story. And not a happy one.

You will never be happy if you continue to search for what happiness consists of.

—Albert Camus

Saturday, February 15, 7:02 a.m.
Naked
Just looked in the mirror
Don't like what I see

I keep thinking about last night. I'm literally obsessed. My brain is incapable of thinking about anything else. When I woke up, I kept my eyes closed, hoping that what I saw was a dream. But it wasn't. I can't believe I stood there at the dance and watched Brynn and Billy pressed against each other, kissing. True, they weren't kissing full on. No lips. No tongue.

Just cheek. But still, it was at a school dance, so I can only imagine what they must be doing elsewhere.

I can't believe I was just about to ask Billy if he wanted to dance, and I really can't believe I was going to ask him if he wanted to get back together. I'm such an idiot. How did I miss this one? Them getting together doesn't have anything to do with planning a dance or making posters or some stupid article. This is about two things: Boobs. Brynn's. They're bigger than mine. Much bigger. I wonder if Billy has touched them. If he hasn't yet, I bet he'd like to.

Oh, God.

10:17 a.m.

My brain is completely stuck on last night. It's not just that Brynn and Billy kissed. I can't believe Brynn never said a word to me about the fact that she and Billy are a couple now. Was she going to tell me or just wait and let me find out on my own? What happened to *best friends tell each other everything*? Sure, Brynn and I have had our differences, but you'd think she'd tell me something big like that, even if she thought it would upset me. She's usually the poster child for "brutal honesty."

And for that matter, why didn't Billy say anything either? He's never said the first word about any of this. Part of me feels like he would try to deny that he and Brynn are a couple or make it seem like it's no big deal. I can just hear him. *"Aw, April, don't get loco on me here."* But I know what I saw. Brynn and Billy. Kissing. On the dance floor.

But I'm confused. What did Billy mean when he said, *"I miss this"*? I thought he was flirting with me. Obviously he wasn't. I don't know.

10:23 a.m.

Actually, I do. It meant nothing.

2:35 p.m.

Brynn just called. That sounds like a good thing, right? It wasn't.

"What happened to you last night?" asked Brynn. "I didn't even see you leave."

I was debating if I wanted to tell Brynn what

I saw or if I wanted to just sit there, not saying anything, to try and force her to admit what happened. Part of me hoped she'd say I might have seen her kiss Billy but it meant nothing. But that's not what happened. Brynn started blabbering on about the dance and how amazing it was and that she had the best time.

She didn't even ask me if I had fun. I guess she knew the answer to that one.

4:15 p.m.

Obsessed

Now my brain is obsessing over something I hadn't thought about until now: how long has this been going on? I don't even want to think about it. But I can't help it. For all I know, Billy and Brynn have been together since New Year's Day when they "hung out" on her bed and watched movies. Brynn and Billy kept secrets about the dance from me. Did they keep other secrets too? I sincerely hope that's not the case, because if it is, the year started off much worse than I even knew.

9:02 p.m.

Sophie just called. She's like a mind reader. "How was the dance?" she asked, and everything spilled out.

"You should call Brynn and talk to her," she said when I was done.

"What would I say? I don't want to sound like a bigger idiot than I already am."

"You say 'I saw you kiss Billy. What's up with that?' Then, you just sit there and wait for her to do the talking," said Sophie.

I grunted into the phone.

Sophie laughed. "This falls into the little stuff category."

Usually what Sophie says makes perfect sense, but I had no clue how she could think my two best friends dating each other falls into the little stuff category.

Nothing about it feels little to me.

Monday, February 17
Study ~~Hall~~ Hell

Today's edition of the *Faraway News* came out at lunch, and Brynn's article about Billy is on the front page along with a big picture of him. I felt sick reading the article. It spilled over onto page two of the newspaper, and when I opened it up, there was a picture of Brynn with her hands on Billy's shoulders, leaning over him while he was writing. The caption under the photo read, "Brynn Stephens, *Faraway News* Editor in Chief, watches as Student Government President Billy Weiss plans the school Valentine's dance." If you ask me, it should have read, "Interviewer getting up close and personal with interviewee."

Brynn is just two desks down from me, and I can't even look in her direction.

10:02 p.m.
Bad day

I didn't speak to Brynn for the rest of the afternoon. The more I thought about the article in the paper and everything that I'm sure has happened between Billy and Brynn that I don't know about, the worse my mood became.

I was leaving after school to go with Emily, Kate, and Vanessa to the community center when Brynn stopped me. "Is something the matter?" she asked. "You haven't said a word to me all afternoon." I really didn't know what to say. Brynn kept talking. "You saw the newspaper article about Billy, right? Don't you think it turned out great?"

I couldn't believe what she was asking me. It was like she was clueless as to how I might be feeling. "I have to get to the community center," I told Brynn and hurried off, but when I got there, my day just got worse.

"So what happened at the dance?" Des asked. I think she could tell by my expression that it didn't go well. "Maybe we should get to work," she said when I didn't answer her question.

"That's a good idea." Ms. Baumann, who I hadn't even seen, was standing behind us. She pulled me aside. "April, your student doesn't appear to be ready for the show."

Not what I wanted to hear from Ms. Baumann.

I've had enough of this day. I'm going to bed.

Tuesday, February 18, 7:54 p.m.

It's possible I'm suffering from chronic bad mood.

When I got home from the community center, May and June had a blanket and pillows set up on the floor in front of the TV. "Want to come to our SpongeBob picnic?" May asked.

"Mom said we can eat dinner in front of the TV!" June was bouncing up and down while she was talking. Even though I could tell they were really into it, I just shook my head like I was RSVPing *no* to their picnic.

As I started walking to my room, Mom stopped me and asked if everything was OK. I told her it was, but it's not. Sophie texted me twice tonight and now she just called. I didn't pick up. I don't want to talk to her about Brynn or Billy or how any of what's happened falls into the small stuff category. Billy called too. I thought about picking up, but I didn't. I've been sitting here for the last twenty minutes, staring at my phone, which put me in an even worse mood.

Which I didn't think was possible.

I don't go looking for trouble.
Trouble usually finds me.

—Harry Potter

Thursday, February 20, 1:37 p.m.
Study Hall

I've managed to avoid Brynn all week. I haven't returned any of her texts or phone calls. I haven't felt like talking to her. But today, I didn't have a choice. She came up to me after assembly. "You haven't spoken to me all week. I texted you last night and you didn't even text back." She was shifting from foot to foot while she talked, which is what she does when she's nervous.

I thought about Sophie's insistence that I say something. "I saw you kiss Billy at the dance."

The words just tumbled out.

Brynn's forehead crinkled up like she was confused. "It was just a kiss between friends."

"A kiss between friends?" It sounded more like a question when I repeated it. I knew I sounded like June, but I didn't care.

Brynn nodded her head. "No big deal."

And that's when I lost it. I didn't want to have a confrontation at school, but everything I'd been feeling and thinking came out. "It was a big deal to me. You're supposed to be my best friend. You and Billy and I are all supposed to be best friends. I know you like Billy, but you haven't said the first word about it to me, and now you're telling me that kissing him was no big deal?" My lips were starting to tremble.

Brynn stood there silent for long time. Whenever we have an issue, she's always defensive. This time was no exception. "April, there's nothing going on between Billy and me."

That wasn't an answer to my question. "You're so into 'brutal honesty' but you can't even admit that you like Billy?"

I waited for Brynn to confirm what we both

knew was the truth, but she didn't do that. "I think we need to take a break," said Brynn.

I nodded.

I couldn't have agreed more.

9:45 p.m.

In my room

Billy just called. He didn't waste any time on small talk. "What's going on with you? You haven't picked up when I've called, and I know you and Brynn had a fight at school."

I wasn't sure if I wanted to say: I saw you kissing at the dance. Or: I thought it seemed like you wanted to get back together. Or even: Funny how neither you nor Brynn mentioned anything to me about how you're a couple now. So all I said was, "Everything's fine."

Billy hesitated, like he was thinking before he spoke. "It just seems like you've been upset all week." He paused. "I guess I just want to know what you're thinking."

"Nothing," I lied. I know I could have said that I don't like it when he and Brynn kiss, or when he says things like *"I miss this."* But I didn't say any of that. Billy hates it when I won't tell him what's on my mind.

It felt incredibly satisfying to just stay quiet.

Friday, February 21, 6:03 p.m.
Big problems

Brynn and Billy are the least of my problems. Even though Brynn and I aren't speaking and Billy's upset because I won't tell him what's on my mind, my biggest problem is Des. Today as I was helping her into her costume for dress rehearsal, which is tomorrow, I could see tears welling up in her eyes. "What's the matter?" I asked.

"I'm not ready for the show." I looked at poor Des, and her face said it all. Tomorrow is dress rehearsal, and she didn't feel confident. She was scared.

"You'll be OK," I said to Des. But my words sounded weak, even to me.

Saturday, February 22
Dress rehearsal disaster

My problems continue to multiply. Dress

rehearsal was a complete disaster for Des. When she was supposed to go left, she went right. When she should have gone right, I don't know where she went. It's not a competition, but most of the other girls looked better than she did. When we were done going through the show, Ms. Baumann pulled me aside. "April, you need to do something."

Clearly.

3:45 p.m.
Back from the diner

I went to the diner to talk to Dad. I had to talk to somebody, and his years of writing an advice column for the Faraway newspaper have always made him a better-than-average choice in my mind. When I got there, he was already in his office. He looked up when he saw me. "April," he smiled. "What brings you here?" He knows the only reason I'd come to the diner on a Saturday afternoon is because I needed to talk.

I sat down in a chair and took a Tootsie Roll out of the bowl on his desk. He didn't say a word while I chewed and swallowed. I got straight to the point. "Brynn and I both like Billy."

Dad raised an eyebrow like he wanted me to elaborate, so I did. I told him everything that happened. When I was done, he sat for a minute with his lips pursed, like he was thinking. Then he spoke. "You know, you're not the first set of friends to fight over a guy," he said.

I hadn't expected that. "Can you give me an example of someone else?"

"Angelina and Jen fought over Brad."

I shook my head. "I don't think they were ever friends."

Dad nodded like I had a point. I asked for another example. Dad furrowed his brow. "I read somewhere that Taylor Swift and Selena Gomez fought over Justin Beiber."

It sounded so funny coming out of Dad's mouth. I laughed out loud. "Where'd you get that?" I asked.

Dad grinned. "I've got my sources." Then he got up and left his office. When he came back, he had two slices of chocolate pie. He handed me a fork, and I dug in.

It didn't solve my problems, but it made me feel a little better.

9:45 p.m.
Some perspective to go with my pie

Tonight I realized my problems aren't nearly as bad or as important as I think they are. I feel sick after what happened today. But not for me. For Matt.

Tonight, when I took Gilligan on a walk, I saw Matt outside. I had this weird feeling like he was waiting to see if I came out, because right when I did, he fell in step beside me and started talking. "You look pretty bad," he said.

"Thanks," I responded sarcastically. I wasn't thrilled about him seeing me with dirty hair, no makeup, and baggy sweatpants.

Matt smiled. "I didn't mean it like that. What's going on?" He nudged my elbow like he was listening if I wanted to talk, so I did.

I told him what happened with Brynn and Billy at the dance. Then I told him about Des and how she's not ready for the dance show. "I feel terrible. I've been so consumed with my own problems, I haven't been focusing on helping her." He was quiet, so I added what I'd been thinking since this afternoon. "I'm a bad person," I said.

"April, you're not a bad person." Maybe he didn't think so, but I felt like one. I'd let Des down.

Matt was quiet for a long time as we walked. I nudged my elbow into his. "Your turn."

He didn't say anything at first. "There's something I haven't told anyone since I moved to Faraway." The way he looked at me, I knew what he was about to say next was serious. I waited until he was ready to continue.

Matt cleared his throat, like it was hard to get the words out. "My mom and I moved here from California because my dad was . . ." He stopped and looked up at the sky. After a moment, he finished. "He was abusive. It was bad." He paused. I didn't say a word.

Matt kept going. "I wanted to leave for a long time. I kept a map of the United States tucked between my mattress and box spring. Every time my dad hit my mom or me, which was a lot, I'd take out the map and point to a different city. 'We should go here,' I'd say to my mom. She always acted like she was considering my suggestion, but I knew she wasn't going to leave. Then one night, my dad was bad. Real bad. He'd been drinking. He punched me in the face so hard, it busted my nose. I knew it was then or never. When my dad passed out, I took out the map and pointed to Faraway. 'That's where we need to go,' I said to Mom. We quickly packed a bag and left. We never looked back." When Matt finished, he looked at me.

I was shocked. Hearing his story brought tears to my eyes. When I pictured him in California, I imagined him surfing and hanging out on the beach. I never envisioned something like this. Now I understood the questions he'd asked about strangers poking around for information on our street. I just looked at him. I was speechless.

"I've been wanting to tell you that for a while." He shrugged. "I mean, I needed to tell someone, and there's just a feeling I get when I'm around you. Like I can trust you." He paused. "Do you know what I mean?"

I nodded. I knew exactly what he meant. I thought about what Sophie had said about me liking Matt. Suddenly, everything seemed so clear. I dropped Gilligan's leash and wrapped my arms around Matt's neck. I hugged him hard, and he let me.

On the side of my cheek, I could feel his tears running into my own.

I'm just trying to change the world, one sequin at a time.

—Lady Gaga

Friday, February 28, 6:15 p.m.
Day before the show

Every afternoon this week, I stayed after rehearsal and worked with Des. It was Matt's idea. On Sunday, he told me this story about his first baseball coach in California who wouldn't let him leave practice one day until he learned to hit.

"I'll never forget it," Matt told me. "It was just Little League, but he treated it like it was the majors. He made me stay at the field and work on my swing for hours after the other kids had gone home. But somehow that night, I got it. You should make Des practice until she gets it," he said.

So I did. Today (which is good timing because the show is tomorrow), when we'd finished going over all the steps in all of the dances, I high-fived Des. "Looking good!" I said. "You've worked really hard, and I know you're ready. I'm proud of you," I added.

When I said that, Des put her hand on her hip. It reminded me of the first time I'd met her. "I'm proud of you, too," she said.

I grinned. It was such a Des thing to say.

Saturday, March 1, 9:39 p.m.
Big night!

Tonight was the dance show at the community center, and it was amazing.

The girls on the dance team and all of the girls who were performing got to the auditorium early. As I was helping Des into her costume, I could tell she was nervous.

"I look like I've been playing dress-up in my mother's closet." She gestured to her costume, which hung on her small frame, and then looked around at some of the more developed girls who filled out their costumes better than she did.

This was a topic I could help her on. I stuck out my own small chest. "I'm right there with you, sister," I said.

She looked down at my little boobs and cracked up. I was just happy I could help her relax. As I was putting her makeup on, we could see from our spot backstage that the auditorium was filling up fast. "Standing room only," Des said.

I knew it was code speak for *I'm scared out of my mind.*

I wrapped my arm tightly around her. "You're going to be great!" I reminded her how hard she'd worked. When the music started and it was time for the girls to line up on stage for the opening number, Des squeezed my hand. "You got it," I mouthed as she went with the other girls to take her place.

The opening number with all of the girls was pretty smooth. Des slid a few times when she should have shuffled, and once she went left when she should have gone right, but she wasn't the only one who made a few missteps, and honestly, they were pretty minor. When Des came backstage, her eyes met mine. Ms. Baumann had drilled it into the girls that there was to be no talking backstage between numbers, so I gave her a thumbs-up. She knew she'd done her part.

The rest of the show went well too. Des was in one more dance, and then everyone went back on stage for the finale. When it was over, the crowd went crazy. I've never heard so much clapping or cheering. The applause went on for a long time. I could see the girls on stage doing curtsies and bows and grinning like they'd just performed on Broadway. It was awesome seeing them all so happy. What happened after the show was cool too. "I'm a star! I'm a big, shiny star!!" Des screamed when she came backstage.

"I don't know about the big part," I said.

Des threw her arms around me and squeezed hard. It was a big hug for a little girl. "You're the best dance teacher ever," she said, ignoring my last comment.

I laughed. "I'm the only one you've ever had!"

"You're the only one I'm ever going to have," Des said. I put my arm around her. She might not continue dancing, but she really did a good job tonight. She slipped her arm around me. We were standing like that, talking to some of the other girls, when Matt came backstage. I was shocked to see him. I had told him about the show, but I didn't think he'd come.

"Great show!" he said to me. Then he looked at Des. "You must be the mighty Desiree." He gave her a big, white-toothed smile.

"Tell me this is Matt," she whispered into my ear. During our week of private rehearsals, she'd managed to coax the latest boy drama out of me, which included Matt minus a few private details. When I nodded that it was, she put two fingers in her mouth and let out a whistle like she approved. Matt belly-laughed.

"Great job," he told Des.

"That's cool he came," Des said when he left. I nodded that it was. "Do you think Billy and Brynn came?" she asked.

I shook my head. My family had been in the audience, but I knew Billy and Brynn weren't there.

Des could tell talking about it upset me. "No big deal," she said, like she was trying to cheer me up. "Things have a way of working out."

I wasn't quite sure how or if things actually will work out with Billy and Brynn, but somehow hearing her say it made me feel better.

I didn't have time to dwell on what she'd said for long. Parents were coming backstage to congratulate the girls. Ms. Baumann made a nice speech telling them all how great they'd done, and then we had a party with a cake and punch. When it was time to say good-bye, Des kissed me on the cheek. "I'm going to miss you," she said. It made me smile. She's a pretty cool kid.

"I'm going to miss you too," I told Des.

10:17 p.m.

Matt just texted me for the first time ever! It was really sweet. Here's how the conversation went:

Matt: Cool how you helped Des.
Me: Thanks for coming to the show!
Matt: I liked it.

Matt: Dance is cool.

Me: :-)

Matt: Spring break next week.

Me: I can't wait!

Matt: We should hang out.

Me: Sounds like fun!

Matt: :-)

10:32p.m.

Can't sleep

I just called Sophie and told her about Matt coming to the show and how he texted me.

"You and Matt are meant to be together," she said when I was done. A chill ran up my spine. I was thinking about what Des had said about how things have a way of working out, and I wondered if that applied to Matt and me. Sophie interrupted my thoughts.

"Did you hear what I said? You and Matt are meant to be together."

I nodded into the phone. Sometimes Sophie can be a little intense, but she's usually right.

Sunday, March 2, 5:18 p.m.
Day of surprises

Billy called this morning and asked if I would come over to his house. I had no idea why he wanted me to. We've barely spoken since the dance. To be fair, he tried to find out what was wrong, but he stopped trying, so I couldn't imagine that he was going to start again now.

When I got to his house, I found out why he called. I wasn't the only one Billy had asked to come over. Brynn was there too. I had no idea he had asked her to come over, and from the look on her face, I don't think she knew I was going to be there either. I could tell she was just as uncomfortable as I was. We haven't spoken in over two weeks. But the minute I got there, Billy made us both sit down, and he started talking.

"We've all been best friends since third grade." He paused like he wanted the weight of that to sink in. "I don't know quite what's happened lately." Brynn and I looked at each other when he said that. Billy didn't miss the animosity between us. "OK, I think I have an idea," he said. "And I don't like it. We need to put the drama behind us and get back to all being friends."

I didn't say anything, and neither did Brynn. Billy looked at both of us like our reaction, or lack of it, was frustrating to him. "I didn't want to come right out and ask this, but you're not leaving me a choice." He paused. "Have you been fighting over me?"

It sounded kind of conceited coming out of his mouth and actually a little bit funny. I guess Billy thought so too, because he smiled and added, "I can't imagine why. But here's the deal: we're all friends, and we're all going to stay friends. No one will be more." He looked at me. "We've tried it, and it didn't work out." I grimaced. I knew what he meant, but his words stung. Brynn looked like she was relieved that he didn't think she was the problem. But he turned to her like she wasn't excluded from the blame. "NO one here can be more than friends. We're the Three Musketeers. Always have been. Always will be. Capiche?"

Brynn and I looked at each other and silently nodded. A lot had happened. But I think neither of us wanted to acknowledge that our friendship has changed. I got the sense she wanted to cling to the idea of us being the Three Musketeers just as much as I did.

"Capiche," I said.

"Capiche," repeated Brynn.

Billy grinned. I could tell he was pleased with his diplomacy skills—and with his next move. He brought out popcorn, mini Reese's, and lemonade, which we all agreed were just as perfect as when we decided they were our snacks of choice, way back in third grade.

The only way to get rid of a temptation is to yield to it.

—Oscar Wilde

Monday, March 3, 3:45 p.m.
Spring Break
Not off to a great start

Matt texted me after lunch and asked if I wanted to hang out at his house and watch a movie. We sat side by side on his couch for ninety-four minutes watching *Anchorman*. He still had on his baseball clothes from practice this morning. He smelled like a field, but I liked it. We laughed the whole time, but what we didn't do was kiss. Our legs were literally side by side, and I kept thinking that at any minute, Matt was going to put his hand on my knee and lean over and kiss me. OK. I'll admit it: I wanted him to. I tried to send vibes to lean over and do it, but he didn't. When the movie ended, he stood up and stretched. "Thanks for coming over," he said like it was time for me to go, so I did.

Ugh! One question: why didn't he kiss me?

6:29 p.m.

It was really bothering me that Matt didn't kiss me so I called Sophie to ask her why she thinks he didn't. "Simple," she said. "He wants to create sexual tension."

I laughed like that explained it, but when I hung up I had to look it up on Urban Dictionary. It said, *The tension felt between two people who want to do something sexual together but hold back.*

Seriously? It was kind of gross reading about it. I'm not even sure kissing qualifies as "something sexual," and I'm really not sure that was what Matt was doing.

Sometimes Sophie really can be weird.

Tuesday, 4:32 p.m.

I'm tossing Sophie's sexual tension theory out the window. I didn't hear from Matt all day. I was hoping I would, as I spent most of the day in my PJs watching cartoons with May and June and eating stale cereal. By 2:00, when I hadn't heard from him, I took the highly unexpected step of cleaning up my room. I thought for sure the good karma created from doing something Mom had been asking me to do for weeks would net me a text or a phone call.

But it didn't.

6:02 p.m.

OMG!

Mom didn't ask me to walk Gilligan before dinner, but I did it anyway, hoping I'd see Matt, and I did. He was in his front yard, throwing a Frisbee to his dog. I actually regretted that I'd decided to walk Gilligan, because I didn't want it to seem like I was looking for him, but when Matt saw me, he waved. "I was going to call you tonight," he said from across his yard. I didn't respond. "I was thinking it would be fun to go to the beach tomorrow. You in?" he asked.

I nodded. Thank you, God. Thank you, Gilligan.

Wednesday
Best day ever!

I have so much to write. Today was the best day of my life, and I'm putting down every perfect detail so years from now when I go back and read this (and I know I'll go back and read it), I'll remember every moment.

It started this morning. Matt and I took the bus to the beach. It's weird. I've lived in Faraway my entire life, and I've never taken the bus anywhere. It's not even like I've wanted to. But Matt seemed to know what to do, so I followed his lead. It was fun sitting side by side with him and checking out the other passengers as the bus rattled across Faraway toward the beach. When we got there, with the exception of a few people walking along the shore and a group of old ladies doing tai chi, the beach was pretty much deserted.

"Let's go in," said Matt after we'd put our

stuff down. He motioned toward the water.

He'd seen me in my suit before, but I suddenly felt self-conscious about being alone with Matt and how I looked in my bikini. "It's kind of cold," I said, pulling my sweatshirt in around me.

Matt smiled. "C'mon," he said. "It's not that bad." He peeled off his T-shirt and sneakers. I tried not to react, but it was hard. He looked so cute and boyish standing there in his trunks with his tight abs.

I knew it was my turn. I unbuttoned my jeans and pulled them off. Matt was watching me. As I lifted my sweatshirt over my head, I said a quick prayer that my boobs would grow right there on the spot so that by the time my sweatshirt was off, they would protrude nicely from my top.

"Nice suit," Matt said. Goose bumps were forming on my skin. We stood there for a minute just looking at each other, then Matt took my hand and we ran to the water's edge. I thought he was going to stop when we got there, but he kept going. It was cold, but it didn't seem to bother Matt. He pulled me out until we were waist-deep. "I love the water," said Matt.

I wasn't as comfortable as he was. I could feel the tide pulling me out. I grabbed Matt's arm. "I got you," he said instinctively, then pulled me toward him. His hands encircled my waist. As we moved out deeper, I let the strength of the current push me closer to Matt. My stomach was pressed against his. I felt the muscles in his midsection tighten. A warmth spread through me despite the cold water. It was like nothing I'd ever felt before.

"April." Matt whispered my name. His face was inches from mine. I could feel his breath on my skin. Then his mouth was pressed against mine and we were kissing. Softly at first. Then Matt's grip tightened around me. Unlike the last time we'd kissed, this time his tongue easily slid into my mouth. My arms found their way around Matt's neck as the warmth of his tongue pressed against mine and his fingers tensed up on the small of my back. I don't know how long we kissed like that, but as the current started to push us out, Matt pulled away. "We better go in," he said hoarsely.

When we got back to where we'd left our belongings on the beach, my skin was covered in goose bumps. I shivered. Even though the sun had started to warm the day, it was still chilly outside. Matt took a towel out of his bag and dried my arms and back, then laid it out on the sand. "C'mon." He gestured to the towel. "Let's dry off for a while." Matt lay down, and I lay next to him. I was a little afraid he was going to pull me on top of him and try to kiss me like that. I wasn't sure I was ready for that. But Matt just stretched out his arm and motioned for me to put my head on it and use it like a pillow. We lay next to each other like that for a long time. Neither of us said a word. We didn't need to. It was just sun and sand and peace and quiet. I'm sure it was the definition of Zen, and I loved it. When it was time to go, Matt propped himself up on his elbows and looked down at me. "You're cute, California."

I grinned. It was the first time he'd called me that in a long time.

As great as the day had been so far, the best thing happened on the bus on the way home. I'll never forget it. Matt took a pen out of his bag and pushed the sleeve of my sweatshirt up over my elbow. "Close your eyes."

When I did, he started writing.

The pen tickled my skin and I tried to pull my arm away, but Matt kept a firm grip on it as he wrote. "Open your eyes," he said when he finished.

When I looked, I couldn't believe what he'd written. The note on my arm said: *Will you go out with me?* Matt had drawn two boxes with labels under each box—*yes* and *yes*. He handed me a pen. When I checked *yes*, he wrapped his arm around me and took a picture of us with his phone.

Even if he hadn't taken the picture, it would have been a totally memorable day.

Thursday, March 6
An unfortunate follow-up

Matt called and asked if I wanted to come over, which I did. His mom was at work, which was cool because we hung out on his couch, watching game shows and making out. To be honest, we kissed so much that my lips were actually swollen. But I didn't care. I think I could have kept kissing Matt forever.

I know that sounds totally ridiculous, but it's true. All I want to do is kiss Matt. I can't believe I ever felt uncomfortable around him. When I left his house, I actually felt a pain in my chest like I was going to miss him even though I'd spent the last three hours making out with him. Ugh! How could that even be possible? It was an awesome afternoon . . . until I got home.

"Where've you been?" asked Mom when I walked into the house. Her face looked suspicious, like she doubted my whereabouts. I said a quick prayer. *Please don't let my lips look as bad as they feel.* Before I'd left, I'd told Mom I was going to hang out with friends. I hadn't lied, but I'd been intentionally unclear. Sooner or later I was going to have to tell my parents about Matt. "Matt and I are going out," I announced.

Mom nodded for a long time, like it was taking her a while to formulate what she wanted to say next. "Did this happen yesterday when you went to the beach?" she asked.

I nodded. I was glad I'd told Mom where I was going.

"Were you with him again today?" I nodded again. I didn't want to start this relationship off with a lie.

"I see," said Mom. But it didn't seem like she saw at all. Her tone was harsh and clipped, and when Dad came home, they both wanted to talk to me. Privately. I had a bad feeling as I followed my parents down the hall to my room.

"April, there are some rules we need to put into place," said Dad as he closed my door.

"Is this about Matt?" I asked. My parents looked at each other and nodded.

"We need to know whenever you're with him," said Mom.

Dad continued. "We want to know where you're going to be and for how long.

"And what time you will be home," added Mom.

They were a tag team, and they weren't done yet. "You're not allowed to be in your room alone with him," said Mom.

"Or alone at his house," said Dad.

I could feel anger rising inside of me. I couldn't believe what I was listening to. I hadn't done anything wrong, and I felt like I was being punished. The happiness I'd felt when Matt and I were alone together at the beach and today on his couch vanished. "You didn't have any of these *'rules'* when I was going out with Billy," I said to my parents.

They looked at each other, and then Dad looked at me. "Matt's not Billy," he said.

"That's a fact, not a reason," I said to Mom and Dad.

But they just looked at each other and then got up to go. Apparently, for them, it was reason enough.

Friday, March 7, 9:15 pm
Weird day
Weird parents

Matt came over after lunch today. We were hanging out in the backyard (which I thought was a good idea as it didn't violate any of Mom and Dad's three billion rules), and May and

June were actually out there with us. Matt pushed them both on the swings until they couldn't go any higher. They were laughing and having fun. Everything was great until I said, "My turn." Then Matt started pushing me, and the minute he did, Mom came outside. She was like the swing police.

She motioned for me to come down. "Your father is coming home from the diner early, and we're going to have a family outing," she announced in this weird, formal way. Then she looked at Matt. "I'm sorry, Matt, but you'll have to go."

Matt shook his head politely, like it wasn't a problem. "It's OK," he whispered in my ear as he left, but it wasn't OK for me.

When Dad got home we went on our "family outing," which was a drive down a country road. In the history of Sinclair family outings, we'd never taken a drive down a deserted road. The more cows we passed, the madder I got. "I know you did this just so I couldn't be with Matt," I said from the backseat.

I saw Mom and Dad glance at each other in the rearview. "That's not true," said Dad.

"You're lying," I mumbled.

"April!" Dad said my name sharply. May and June scooted away from me, like they didn't want to be part of what was happening. That made me even madder. They're my sisters, so they're supposed to be on my side, and they were having fun when Matt pushed them on the swings this morning.

I poked May in the leg. "Tell Mom and Dad how nice Matt is. Tell them that he pushed you on the swing and how much fun it was." I knew my voice had a sharp tone, but I couldn't help it. May was quiet. I poked her again. "Go on. Tell them," I said.

"Matt's OK," she said quietly. "But I like Billy better." Her voice was almost inaudible. June looked out the window.

For once, she wasn't going to repeat what she heard, even though her body language made it pretty clear she felt the same way. Mom and Dad looked at each other. They heard what was being said. And what wasn't.

Saturday, March 8
Started out weird
Ended happy

Billy called early this morning. "What's up? I haven't seen you all week."

"I've just been hanging out," I said. I knew it sounded lame, but I wasn't ready to tell him about Matt. It hadn't gone well when I'd told my family. I couldn't image how Billy and Brynn would react.

"What do you say you, Brynn, and me go on a bike ride tomorrow?" I didn't answer right away. I wasn't sure that was what I wanted to do.

"C'mon," said Billy. "It'll be fun." I knew I couldn't say no. I also knew that sooner or later I'd have to tell my friends about Matt. And sooner was probably better than later. At least they'd have time to digest it before we go back to school.

So Brynn and I met at Billy's, and we went on the bike ride we've done together so many times before. We rode to Rock Creek, then on to Mr. Agee's farm, and we finished our ride with Slurpees at 7-Eleven, just like we've always done. As we sat down on the curb to drink them,

I knew it was time to say something.

I waited for the sugary rush from the Slurpee to go to my head. "I have an announcement to make." It sounded overly dramatic, even to me. Brynn and Billy stopped drinking and looked at me. Anxiety coursed through me. I started talking before I could chicken out. "Matt and I are going out." I said. The words sat on the curb like a divider between us. No one said anything. Finally, Brynn broke the silence.

"Do you think that's a good idea?" she asked, like she didn't.

"Matt's nice." I tried to keep my voice steady. I didn't want to seem defensive.

Brynn shook her head like she disagreed with my choice of adjectives. I didn't want to get emotional, but I could feel tears welling up in my eyes. Billy could tell I was upset.

He put an arm around me. "Trust your judgment." He managed to sound diplomatic and reassuring at the same time, even though I'm sure it wasn't easy for him. Then he squeezed my shoulder. It seemed like his way of saying he'd always be there for me.

When we finished drinking our Slurpees, we pedaled home. As I left them behind at Billy's and rode home, I kept thinking about that conversation. Billy had made it easy. He's always a gentleman. Brynn's reaction was annoying, but it was what I expected. It sucks that she couldn't just be happy for me. I know we're growing apart, and it makes me sad.

When I got home, I called Sophie. She'd been in France all week, so I hadn't been able to tell her about getting together with Matt. She started screaming into the phone—in French!

"Huh?" I laughed. I had no clue what Sophie had said.

"I'm sooooooo happy for you!" she explained.

Hearing her voice, and having someone be happy for me—even in another language—made me smile bigger than I had all day.

Everybody has their own path.
It's laid out for you.
It's just up to you to walk it.

—Justin Timberlake

Sunday, March 9, 9:45 p.m.
Last night of spring break

Tonight I went to Gaga and Willy's for dinner. My whole family was there, and the main topic of conversation was me. Mom must have told Aunt Lilly and Aunt Lila about Matt, because all night they kept "teasing" me—or harassing me, depending on how you look at it—about my new boyfriend.

"April, we hear Matt's a real cutie pie," said Aunt Lilly.

"A ninth grader! Wowsa!" said Aunt Lila.

Wowsa? I could feel myself getting annoyed, and dinner hadn't even started yet. I knew my aunts weren't really impressed that Matt's cute or in ninth grade. All the stuff they were saying was a cover for what they were really trying to do, which was to find out information for Mom, who I'm sure told them she's worried about me going out with Matt. And they weren't the only ones talking about my relationship.

Harry, who is in tenth grade and knows Matt from school, had a lot to say about him too. Actually, he didn't have much to say, but what he said made an impact.

"Matt's an asshole," Harry announced.

Unfortunately, it made my aunts try even harder than they already had to get information out of me. Aunt Lila took my hand like we were buddies and we had to talk. "So tell us all about him," she said.

I snatched my hand away. I didn't want to talk about Matt—I wanted to defend him. "How do you know Matt's an asshole?" I asked Harry. "Are you friends? Have you ever hung out with him? Do you even know him?"

Mom didn't give Harry a chance to answer. She nodded toward my cousins Charlotte and Izzy, who are five. "April, let's not use profanity in front of your cousins."

"Harry used it first," I said. All I did was repeat what he'd said, which was an unfair thing for him to say in the first place. I didn't think I should be getting blamed for anything here when the people who deserved the blame were the ones getting into my business for no good reason. I tried to change the subject at that point.

"It's pretty cold for early March," I said. I would have much rather talked about the weather than about Matt, but no one seemed to want to talk about anything other than him.

"Can I see a picture of him?" Amanda asked. I couldn't very well say no, so I pulled out my phone and showed her the one Matt took of us on the bus. Everyone crowded around like I had a picture of the president on my phone. My aunts, Mom, Harry, Charlotte, and Izzy all wanted to see. Somehow Gaga had gotten into the mix too.

"You're pretty cozy there," Aunt Lila said when she saw the picture.

"He's hot," said Amanda.

"He sure is!" Gaga put her fingers between her teeth and whistled.

Izzy laughed.

"If I had a boyfriend like that, I'd want to get cozy too," said Amanda.

Aunt Lilly looked like she was about to explode. She shook a finger at Amanda like she didn't approve of her daughter talking that way. Then she looked at me and made a *tssk* sound, like the direction the conversation had taken was my fault.

But I hadn't done anything wrong! I'm not the one who started the conversation, and it wasn't my fault that Amanda expressed an opinion. She has an opinion on everything.

I'd had just about all I could take. I could feel tears forming in the corners of my eyes. I tried to blink them back. It was the last night of spring break, and I'd come to Gaga's to eat grilled steak, not be grilled about my new boyfriend.

Then something shocking happened. Gaga came to my defense. I think she could tell that I was upset. She wrapped an arm around me.

"When I was your age," she said loudly, like she was talking to me but wanted the whole group to hear what she had to say, "I had my first boyfriend."

"This is April's second boyfriend," Amanda interjected.

Gaga ignored her and kept going. "In matters of the heart, there is only one person you need to listen to." She squeezed my shoulders and looked at me directly. "Only you can know how you truly feel about another person, and that's what matters most. Sometimes you have to take a chance on relationships."

Then she looked at everyone who was gathered around like she was done talking to me and was now addressing them. "You have to block out what others have to say and do what you think is right for you." When she finished her speech, I wanted to salute her.

Bravo Gaga!

Everyone was quiet. Gaga just stood there, like she wanted the full effect of what she'd said to sink in. Then she announced that dinner was served.

So I sat down with my family and ate steak with sautéed mushrooms. I'm not sure if it was the delicious dinner or Gaga's wise and protective words that made me so happy, but a warm, relaxed feeling spread through me like the melting butter on the steak.

"Delicious dinner," my Uncle Drew said to Gaga.

"Thank you." Gaga looked pleased with herself. "I used a recipe tonight."

Everyone chuckled. Sometimes Gaga cooks with recipes, but more often than not, she's what she calls a creative cook. She likes to "make it up as she goes along." Sometimes the results are good, but sometimes they're not.

I had the thought that life would be a lot easier if it came with a recipe—an instruction manual on how to do things, like tell if your best friend likes your boyfriend, or in this case, your ex-boyfriend, or how to tell if he still likes you, and most importantly, how to tell if the hot guy next door likes you as more than a friend.

That would definitely simplify things.

It's crazy—just a few months ago, I was so sure I wanted to get back together with Billy. But now I know I wanted it for the wrong reasons. I think Sophie had it right. Maybe it was because I didn't want Billy to be with Brynn, or because I wanted him to always be there for me. Maybe it was a little of both.

But it doesn't matter. Sometimes it's just hard to separate friendship from something more. And for that matter, it's hard to deal with friendships as they change. It makes me sad that Brynn and I don't see eye to eye like we used to. Hopefully, we can get back there again.

And then there's Matt.

I get why my parents are worried. Matt's older, and they don't really know him. Not like they knew Billy. I guess that's the problem May and June and even Brynn have too—they just don't know Matt. But I know him. And I like him. A lot.

Going out with him makes me feel like there are all kinds of possibilities, a whole world just waiting for me to explore it. Gaga said only I can know what's right for me, and what feels right for me is Matt Parker. I'm trusting my heart.

It seems like a very Zen thing to do.

About the Author

Laurie Friedman remembers what it felt like to be torn between two boys in middle school. One Valentine's Day, she went through a whole box of candy hearts hoping to gain some insight into her true feelings. She remembers it as tasty but unhelpful.

Ms. Friedman is the author of *Can You Say Catastrophe?* and *Too Good to Be True*, the first two books in the Mostly Miserable Life of April Sinclair series. She is also the author of the award-winning Mallory series as well as many picture books, including *I'm Not Afraid of this Haunted House*; *Love, Ruby Valentine*; *Thanksgiving Rules*; and *Back to School Rules*. She lives in Miami with her family. You can find Laurie B. Friedman on Facebook, Pinterest, and Twitter, or at www.lauriebfriedman.com.

Is there any silver lining when you're born into what is clearly the wrong family?

April Sinclair sure hopes so!

Ten Reasons My Life Is Mostly Miserable

1. My mom: Flora.
2. My dad: Rex.
3. My little sister: May.
4. My baby sister: June.
5. My dog: Gilligan.
6. My town: Faraway, Alabama.
7. My nose: too big.
8. My butt: too small.
9. My boobs: uneven.
10. My mouth. Especially when it is talking to cute boys.

THE MOSTLY MISERABLE LIFE OF APRIL SINCLAIR

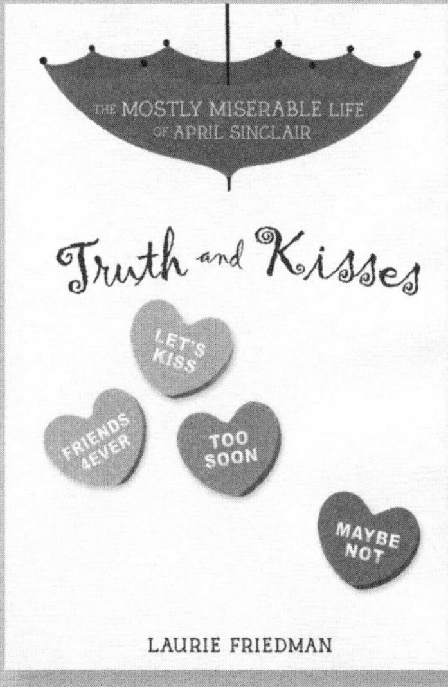